BEDEVILED

B H CARTER

Contents

INTRODUCTION

This book is written with the understanding that life is about a spiritual journey that is both personal and public. This spiritual journey begins with events in our lives, meeting specific individuals, being at a particular place at an exact time, and seeing our lives move in different and unexpected directions.

Although a fiction novel, this book is based on the author's personal experiences and does not intend to infer that everyone experiences the same spiritual awakening. It is the author's opinion that there are good and evil in the world, that there is a heaven and a hell, and that one makes personal decisions that impact all areas of their life.

The author does not render spiritual, emotional, or professional advice. The author asserts that all characters are fictional and any similarity to actual individuals is coincidental and not to be construed as the author engaging in micro-scoping or categorizing characters.

The author disclaims any liability, loss, or risk, personal or otherwise, which is incurred as a consequence, directly or indirectly, of the reading of this book.

CONNECT WITH THE AUTHOR

Website: www.bhcarterauthor.com
Email: barbara@bhcarterauthor.com
Instagram: www.instagram.com/bh_carterauthor
Twitter: www.twitter.com/bh_Carterauthor
FB: www.facebook.com/BHCarterMinistry

Chapter One

SADISTIC BEHAVIOR

After getting Scotty's number, it was a month before I called. Looking back, it was one of the biggest mistakes I have ever made.

My body still shudders from the memory as I reflect on the phone call from Adelai that night. I ignored the obvious signs flashing before my face.

Several months into my and Scotty's relationship, as I prepared for bed, my heart rate and breath raced as if fleeing from an attacker, an uneasy feeling gnawing in my spirit. Hoping to be energetic and enthusiastic for work on Monday morning, I got in bed at 9:00 p.m. Hours later, when the drone of the ringing telephone startled me, I jolted upright and glanced at the time. *Midnight? It must be the wrong number. No one calls me in the middle of the night.*

I closed my eyes and drifted back to sleep. The buzzing from the telephone sounded far away, as if in my neighbor's home, but it got louder and closer, waking me a second time. Rolling onto my side, I fumbled for the landline phone, wondering who could be calling at this time of the night.

"Hello…" I mumbled lazily.

"Hannah, this is Adelai. You won't believe what your boyfriend did to Lenny." Adelai gasped as though she had just finished a marathon and described every detail that had happened earlier in the day, ending with the statement, "That old man you're dating tried to run Lenny off the road and almost killed him!"

I heaved, rubbed my eyes, and sat on the side of the bed. "What? Scotty almost killed Lenny. What happened?"

"Well," Adelai stammered, "He didn't almost kill Lenny, but he ran him off the road. He could have been killed if Lenny wasn't such a good driver."

Any dregs of sleep were now gone, and I was wide awake. "Tell me what happened, Adelai."

"I am. Be quiet and listen."

A wide yawn escaped my mouth, and I exhaled, preparing to listen to every word, blacking out any thoughts that couldn't be true.

"Lenny was going to pick up pizza at Jimmy's on Broadway. You know how Broadway merges into one lane when you reach 51st Street, right?"

"Yes."

"Well, Lenny was driving in the right lane and had the right of way. The stop light was yellow, and Lenny said he had cruised through the light. As he was driving up the hill, merging into the single lane, out of nowhere, a black Toyota SUV sped past him from the left lane. Lenny swerved onto the shoulder, barely missing the drop off into the sewer, to avoid colliding with the black SUV. Lenny was furious, so he followed the SUV up to 60th, which branched back into two lanes."

"Okay. What does this have to do with Scotty? He doesn't have a black Toyota SUV."

Adelai said in a high-pitched voice. "I'm getting to that if you just listen and stop interrupting me."

I blew into the receiver. "I'm sorry. I won't say another word until you finish."

"Lenny pulled up in the right lane next to the black SUV, blew his horn, rolled his window down, and was about to curse the driver out. He shouted, 'You almost ran me off the road! I could have ended up in that sewer. Roll your window down so I can see who I'm talking to.' You won't believe what happened next."

"What happened?"

"Lenny said the driver slowly rolled the window down on the passenger side, and he saw 'your' Scotty. When Scotty stared at him with a close-lipped smile and tucked chin, Lenny was speechless. The light changed when Lenny regained his voice, and Scotty sped away without saying he was sorry."

"What time did this happen? Why are you just calling me now?"

"Lenny didn't tell me at first. He knew I would call and tell you. Girl, you know how men are; they like to handle their business themselves. Lenny returned home around 10:00 p.m., so it happened around 9:00 p.m. tonight."

The back of my neck tightened like a coiled rope, and I caressed it to remove some of the tension. "I don't know what to say, Adelai. I'm sorry that this happened to Lenny." My brows creased, and I twisted my lips from left to right. "What do you want me to do about it?"

Adelai shouted, "Talk to that fool! I don't want a war to start with him and Lenny. You know how Lenny is. He talked about blowing Scotty's head off until I calmed him down. You and I know nothing is happening with you and Lenny, but your old man thinks Lenny wants you. Lenny doesn't want to be looking over his shoulder, wondering if Scotty is around waiting to attack him." She paused. "I think Lenny is a little scared of Scotty. He didn't say it, but I know Lenny. That's why I'm calling you. I convinced him that you needed to know what type of fool you are dealing with."

My face flushed, and anger rose when she called my man a fool, but I held it at bay. I didn't know what to say, so I said nothing, the coiled rope moving from my neck to the rest of my body.

We listened to each other's inhalations and exhalations for several beats while waiting for the other to speak. I waited for Adelai to say more, and she apparently expected me to respond. No words of explanation came into my head, and I did not know what else to say. Was I appalled that Scotty tried to run Lenny or anyone off the road? Definitely, and I didn't want to believe it. But I had known Adelai and Lenny for many years and knew they wouldn't make up a story like this.

Adelai finally spoke, her voice trembling. "Hannah, I'm also concerned about you. What will he do to you if you ever try to break up with him?"

Quiet still filled the atmosphere, but I pondered her question this time. Would Scotty be one of those men who says if I can't have you, no one else will have you if we break up?

"Hannah," Adelai called my name and waited. "Are you listening?"

"I'm here." I hoped she didn't hear the distress in my voice as I chewed my lip and rocked on the side of the bed.

"Be careful. If Lenny is scared, there is something more to Scotty than meets the eye. I've gotta go. I'll talk to you later, okay?"

"Okay." As I hung up the phone, thinking about Adelai's story, I was still at a loss for words.

Unable to fall asleep, I tossed and turned, thinking back on my and Scotty's relationship. What had I missed? Scotty attended church every Sunday, held doors open for other women and me, tipped service workers twenty to twenty-five percent, and showed himself to be a compassionate, generous gentleman. I couldn't believe he would try to run anyone off the road. It must have been an accident, I thought.

That had to be it. It was an accident, and Lenny imagined that it was on purpose. Why would he and Adelai even think that Scotty would do such a thing? I stored the incident in my subconscious and decided not to mention it to Scotty.

How do you bring something like that up to your man? How do you tell the man you are engaged to marry that your friend accused him of running her boyfriend off the highway? Especially a man who talks the most during conversations, confronts teen boys littering his neighborhood, and persuades most people to agree with his position.

I splayed my fingers over my eyes with one hand. "The first thing Scotty will say is that it's 'hear-say.'" He had told me multiple times that he didn't like 'hear-say' information and didn't want others butting in our business.

I can hear him in my head now, "Why did they tell you and not bring it to me if they're accusing me? I hate a coward. I told you, Hannah, at the beginning of our dating that we would do fine in our relationship if we don't let third parties meddle in our business."

I buried the incident and tried to forget it, but any emotions of sadness, anger, anxiety, and stress overtook me and showed on my face or in my behavior. I definitely didn't have a poker face. That Saturday, while eating breakfast at Denny's, Scotty picked up that something was bothering me.

"What's wrong, Hannah?" He leaned closer to the table and looked into my eyes.

"Nothing." My head tilted toward the table, and I pretended to read the menu. "I just have a lot on my mind."

He wouldn't accept "nothing" for an answer and asked, "What's on your mind?" compassion sounded in his voice as he steepled his fingers and moved his head closer to mine.

"Just work stuff." Attempting to change the subject and take the focus off of me, I asked, "What are you having for breakfast this morning?"

Scotty began guessing what the problem could be. After asking what was happening at my job, family, finances, and church, he gruffly stated, "I know you, Hannah. I know your every mood and that something is bothering you. You might as well tell me because I will keep asking and guessing until you do."

After a deep inhale, I decided to take a risk and told him what Adelai had shared about him trying to run Lenny off the road.

As I expected, he hit the table, his jaws clenched, and his face flushed. "Why are you bringing this up to me, Hannah? I told you we would get along fine if we didn't let a third party dabble in our business. Why wasn't the dude man enough to come to me with it rather than running to you? I thought you said you and he didn't see each other?"

Scotty was a genius at turning things around and making the other person the culprit. The conversation suddenly switched from me being upset to Scotty being incensed about Lenny and me seeing each other. I quickly replied, "I didn't see him! If you *really* listened to me instead of looking for opportunities to accuse me, you would have heard me say that Adelai called and told me." My lips pressed together, and my body twitched.

"I'm going to kick that Negro's butt the next time I see him."

Realizing Scotty was at his 'not listening' level, I sighed, and for the remainder of breakfast, I soothed and calmed him, saying, "You're a good man, and I know you wouldn't do anything like that. I don't know why Lenny thought it was you, but it's okay because we won't let it affect us." I held his hand. "And we're not going to let third parties interfere in our relationship."

He never admitted or denied the accusation, and we never discussed the incident again.

For hours after returning home, I sat at my bay window staring at the brightly colored lilies, tulips, and daffodils, trying to figure out how I got intimately involved with Scotty Brian. What made me stay with him after Adelai told me about his sadistic behavior? What spell did he have on me that I excused the incidents of outrage, verbal abuse, degradation, and insane jealousy he displayed?

Chapter Two

THE BEGINNING

L ike a smooth, flowing stream, the sound of a calm, soft, and soothing voice calling my name brought me back to the present and away from the memories of past years.

"Hannah. Hannah? You started telling me how you met your husband, and then you blanked out and stared into space. Are you okay?"

The plush, brown leather armchair caressed my body as I leaned back into it and stared at Dr. Joyce, the psychiatrist I was seeing. *How did I end up here?*

Images of the many mistakes and wrong choices of men I made between the ages of thirty and forty when I was supposed to be more intelligent, wiser, and a better judge of character floated through my head. My first marriage in my twenties and the volatile relationship with physical fights and hateful name-calling, I chalked up to immaturity. I had found the courage to end it and thanked God for a wonderful son from the union.

My shoulders slumped, and I buried my face in my hands, wiping away tears with my knuckles. I asked myself how and why I waited until my forties to allow a man to manipulate, control, misuse, and verbally and emotionally abuse me. Condemnation and regret smothered me with thoughts that I should have used godly wisdom in my relationships and should have been wise enough not to be taken advantage of by a man. *How in the world did I end up marrying such an evil and demon-possessed man?*

Several years after divorcing my son's dad, I longed to marry a man who loved, cherished, and adored me. I loved the institution of marriage, and my heart pined whenever I watched couples interacting, imagining me and my husband caressing, smiling, and gazing into each other's eyes. When Scotty Brian entered my life, I just knew God had answered my prayer for a husband.

Dr. Joyce waited patiently and studied me while I wrapped my arms around my shoulders and rocked, gathering my thoughts.

Here I sat in a psychiatrist's office whimpering, dreadlocks needing grooming, clothes wrinkled, black circles underneath my eyes from lack of sleep, and putting myself down mentally. From my teen years, I always presented myself as fashionable and well-put-together. Mother did not let us leave the house with wrinkles, uncombed hair, or not bathed.

Not wanting to look into the doctor's eyes, fearing that a look of pity would gaze back at me, I continued staring down. *What is wrong with me that I select the terrible men? How did I allow myself to get into this condition I'm in now?*

Dr. Joyce cleared her throat and interrupted my thoughts again. "Tell me, Hannah, how did you meet and marry your husband?"

Here starts my story of how I met and allowed Satan to bedevil me into marrying the man I later felt was Satan's son.

My full name is Hannah Marie Cotton. In 1997, after Scotty spotted me at the performance of CATS at the Majestic Theater, he asked me out. I finally agreed to go out with him, and his confidence, intelligence, and fatherly protection charmed me. One outing led to multiple dates, our engagement, and marriage. The theater was an un-usual place to meet men since their wives or girlfriends accompanied most. The chance meeting prompted me to think the connection was from God and that destiny chose Scotty as my husband.

That evening, the sky was angelic, baby blue with white, fluffy clouds floating in space and the temperature in the high 70s, a beautiful summer evening for late August in the Midwest. My two best friends and I headed to the theater to connect with the rest of our group. Unable to sit together, some women sat in the center aisle, while others sat to the left and right. Outgoing and talkative, I chatted with the ladies behind me, looking back to comment every now and then.

During intermission, I strolled to the ladies sitting to the left and right and hugged the ones I hadn't greeted. I spotted an older man's face turning and following my movements, but I didn't think anything of it because he was old enough to be my dad. After the show ended and we headed out, the man eyeing me said, "Hello," as I passed his seat. I smiled and returned the greeting.

At our next girlfriends' meeting, Adelai informed me that I had an admirer from the theater outing, and he wanted to meet me. Her sister drove for him and his brother, Moses, Transportation Company, and said my admirer liked the classiness of the woman wearing the two-piece, black leather suit. I was flattered because I had prepared for the outing by trimming and tightening my dreadlocks, getting a manicure, pedicure, and even a facial, and I thought I looked attractive in my new suit.

Six single gold buttons ran down the front of the jacket, which tapered at the waist. The skirt was knee-length, split up on the left side, and gold buttons ran from the fork to the core.

I am only describing what I was wearing because Scotty asserts he knew I was a "lady" and wanted to meet me because of how I dressed and sat. I should have discerned an oddity in his character when he said he wanted to meet me because of how I *sat*. Instead, I brushed it off as his unique way of approaching and impressing women.

Adelai and Shirley tried to help me remember the gentleman sitting behind me, but I could not visualize how he looked.

"He was neatly groomed, wearing a tan sports jacket with black pants," said Adelai. "I thought he was kind of handsome."

Shirley added, "He had curly, receding black hair, slightly graying at the temples, pulled back in a ponytail –"

Adelai interjected, "He was about six feet tall, two hundred and forty pounds, with a bulldog face, and he walked with a cane." Her brows creased. "You don't remember the man sitting behind us in the aisle seat?" She laughed. "He stared at you every time you moved."

My lips twisted to one side. "I remember an older man watching me, but I didn't pay that much attention to him." My hands went to my hips. "You said he was handsome; now you're saying he had a bulldog face. Which one is it?"

Adelai thought for a moment. "He wasn't super handsome but wasn't ugly either. I think it was his jowls that made me think of a bulldog."

"That's the man who wants to meet me?"

"Yes." Shirley rolled her eyes and pressed her lips together. "Hannah, you've got to be more observant and watch everything as I do."

"I'm not interested in him. He's old enough to be my daddy."

"He looked to be in his late sixties," Shirley said. "But he looked good for an older man." She threw her head back in laughter.

"He has been pestering my sister all day," said Adelai. "He saw her chatting with you and asked if she knew you."

"I don't remember the man sitting behind us." I yawned. "Girl, I don't want to go out with an 'old' man. I'm only forty."

The rest of the ladies chimed in and discussed the pros and cons of dating older men, many of whom felt older men were more giving, mature, and wealthy and knew what they wanted. They gave me their opinions, and I left the group, determined that I was uninterested in meeting this older gentleman.

Chapter Three

BUYING THE DEVIL'S LIES

For weeks after the theater outing, Scotty sent messages through Adelai that he wanted to meet me. Being the curious, emotional, hopelessly romantic female I am, I began imagining a relationship with Scotty, even though he met none of the requests in my diary. *I think it's sweet that he noticed me sitting and wanted to meet me.*

I reasoned that going on one date with him was no harm. *I'm not going to marry him; it is just a dinner date.*

A plus in Scotty's favor was that I didn't think he was pursuing me for sex as most men my age since he was 25 years older.

Since I wasn't advertising on dating sites searching for a man, and the theater was a strange place for me to meet men, I convinced myself it might be from God for us to get together.

Single for fifteen years and praying to God for a mate, I was ripe as a cherry for Satan's plucking. Shirley and Michelle had married and had their husbands with them at functions, and I was beginning to feel like an outsider. I'm saying that I went out with Scotty because I felt like an intruder being single. In my heart, I knew he was not the partner I had prayed for. I downgraded my criteria and chose a man for myself rather than waiting on God to help my mate find me.

My male friends said I was too picky and should slightly lower my standards. One friend said, "Men want to be needed, and you act like you don't need a man."

Deciding to be less picky and open to going out with a man older and different from my list of qualities that I desired in my husband, I finally said yes to Scotty's date request.

The devil deceived me into thinking Jehovah had sent Scotty. Until I went out with Scotty, Satan repeated in my head, "This man could be sent from God." Considering the words were from the Holy Spirit, I paid attention when the voice said, "I'll give you several reasons why you should believe. You're not looking for a man, content being single, and don't need a man to make you whole. You didn't meet him at a bar but at a *nice* theater. You're following your passion, building a business, and not waiting for your husband to complete you. Establishing intimacy with Jesus is a priority in your life, and you must sacrifice time to build a relationship. Time is tight in your life. Scotty Brian is not the type of guy you're attracted to or would date, but God knows better than you what you need. Jehovah knows you need a mature and settled man."

My plate was packed with growing my business, paying staff to cover the 2nd and 3rd shifts, and working two part-time jobs. And building a relationship took work and time, which I didn't have much of then.

After hearing the whispers in my head for weeks about why I should date Scotty, I concluded that Scotty was a divine connection. I didn't consider that Satan could have sent him.

Working two jobs and trying to build my small business, I didn't have time for much socializing. My business hours were from 6:00 a.m. to 2:00 p.m. Monday through Friday and from 3:00 p.m. to 7:00 p.m. I worked a part-time job at a neighborhood school. A local hospital bought my time every other weekend from 11:00 p.m. to 7:30 a.m. I often worked every weekend at the hospital because of short staffing or the need for extra hands.

Although I was praying to God for a godly mate, I wasn't eyeing every man who smiled at me and thought he might be my spouse. I *thought* I was waiting patiently and faithfully for the husband God was sending my way. A man after God's own heart, saved, sanctified, and anointed, between thirty-eight and forty-eight years old. Handsome, physically fit, hard-working, and honest, he put God first and his wife and family second. He loved, respected, cherished, honored, and desired to protect and provide for me. Our marriage would be anointed and blessed from heaven, and we would only have eyes for each other. We would be compatible emotionally, physically, sexually, spiritually, intellectually, personally, and socially.

Since I was not hunting for a spouse, especially with a man twenty-five years older who didn't meet the requirements for the partner I was praying for, I figured it wouldn't hurt to go to dinner with the gentleman. If he *were* sent from God, I wouldn't miss out on my blessing; if he weren't, it would give me a break from the three jobs.

I phoned Adelai and told her I had changed my mind and would like to meet the man, to get his number, and I would call him.

Chapter Four

ANGEL OF LIGHT

After getting Scotty's number, it was a month before I called. In retrospect, it was one of the biggest mistakes I have ever made. If I had never contacted him, I would not have spent two years with him and wouldn't have married a man I felt was Satan's son. It would be a moot point.

What's the worst that could happen? I telephoned him, and we had an interesting, engaging conversation for an hour. He spoke intelligently and had this deep, rich, strong voice that sounded younger than his age. He focused the discussion on my interests and what I liked to do, and then we discussed our church affiliations; I loved that he attended church twice a week and was a Christian. When asked about previous marriages, he spoke positively of his three ex-wives and an only child, Charlessa.

My brick wall crumbled into stones as we conversed, and he didn't curse, talk about horoscopes or violence against women, or sound like a maniac. Scotty was a good conversationalist, respected my opinions, and did not interrupt when I spoke. After that conversation, I thought he was a caring, sensitive, understanding, and loving man who acted genuinely interested in me.

Satan comes as an angel of light, pretending to be *good* when he is full of *evil*. I should have remembered what the apostle Paul said,

"And no wonder, for Satan himself masquerades as an angel of light. It is not surprising, then, if his servants masquerade as servants of righteousness" II Corinthians 11: 14-15 (NIV).

We talked for two hours in our second conversation, discussing his positions on corporate boards and his community involvement. Each time we chatted, he became more enjoyable and easier to talk to. When I discussed my struggle in building my business, he responded with interest and compassion, offered to assist, gave several suggestions on marketing, and volunteered to present my brochures to his several boards. I was delighted he listened and didn't just hear my words, appreciating him accepting me and considering me attractive. After our second conversation, Scotty moved from a one on my scale to a ten.

After hanging up and staring at the phone, I said, "He can't be that bad if he's this easy to talk to." *Indeed, I would have picked up something about him I didn't like during those two conversations.* He talked favorably about his dead parents and grandparents and appeared to be an excellent dad. Charlessa was the focus of his discussion when he wasn't finding out about me. He talked about how proud he was of her; she was the apple of his eye and the most important person in his life.

I accepted when he asked me out to dinner during our third conversation. It was time to meet this gentleman face to face, who presented himself well and seemed kind and considerate.

We decided on a seafood restaurant on the third Saturday evening in October. Scotty had done his homework and knew my favorite restaurants and the type of food I liked. Adelai said that after spotting me, Scotty badgered her sister with questions about me every day. "What is her favorite color, favorite foods, where does Hannah shop, what size dress does she wear, what type of jewelry does Hannah like, what type of car does she drive, what side of town does she live?"

He discovered that Lake Bistro Seafood Restaurant was my favorite eating establishment. Fortunately, Adelai's sister didn't know enough about me to answer all of his questions, and when she asked Adelai, she refused to provide the information, saying, "He can ask Hannah when he gets to know her."

As the third Saturday in October approached, I was still unsure whether I wanted to go out with an older man, even though I enjoyed chatting with him. He sounded nice over the phone, and we had excellent conversations, but he was not the type of man I was interested in. Twenty-five years older and didn't share the same goals as me. He was retired, and I was starting my own business at the peak of my career. He was slowing down, and I was accelerating. For several hours, I debated whether I should cancel our meeting.

Still undecided, it was five o'clock before I got dressed and headed to the restaurant for our six p.m. reservation. You've heard the old saying, "Curiosity killed the cat." Curiosity and Scotty being an enigma prompted me to have dinner with him. To this day, I wish I had followed my first thoughts, intuition, sixth sense, and the Holy Spirit and not met him on that date. After our first meeting, Scotty stole my mind and heart, bewitching me with his words and gifts.

When I drove up, I spotted an older man wearing tan pants with a navy-blue blazer waiting outside. I knew it was Scotty because the waiting man looked identical to Adelai's description, and he leaned on an ebony wooden cane. A smile crossed my face as my mind thought it courteous of him to wait outside to ensure I got safely inside the restaurant. *He's not that bad looking. It is so sweet of him to wait for me outside, especially since I'm so late.*

He told me years later that he was outside, leaving because he had decided that I wasn't coming. As I got to really, really know Scotty, I discovered he was a liar and said things to humiliate me. When he told me years later that he was not waiting outside for me, he pointed out that I was not a *lady* and was not worth waiting for.

He said, "A lady deserves respect. A woman needs to earn respect." His eyes had squinted, and he turned up his nose. "You are not a lady. When you were nearly an hour late on our first date, I knew you weren't a lady then."

Chapter Five

BEDAZZLED AND DECEIVED

When I approached Scotty under the canopy of the entrance, the carved lion and infinity symbol at the top of his African walking cane glistened underneath the lights.

We headed inside, and when we reached the door, he opened it for me, strolled in after me to the desk, handed the manager a twenty-dollar bill, smiled, and asked if his previous reservation was still available.

The manager added his name to the list and beckoned for a server. The waiter sat us at a table near a window where we watched frothy, white waves from Lake Michigan roll onto the beach, grab a mouth full of pebbles, and roll back into the water. Geese and ducks splashed in the water with their little ones.

Scotty started the conversation by saying he was surprised he had never seen me around town before and asked what I did for fun.

I apologized for being late and then talked about the bowling league I was on for several minutes. I added that I liked to dance, stroll by the lake, and go to live theater performances and concerts when I had time in-between running an Adult Family Home business and working two part-time jobs.

He listened without interrupting as I talked, maintained eye contact, mimicked my body language, responded sensitively, asked many questions about my career, business, part-time jobs, and family, and seemed interested.

As darkness replaced the sunlight, bright streetlights highlighted the several museums in the area, and the quarter moon in the sky glistened.

After smiling, nodding, and offering suggestions, he shared stories of growing up in the thirties and forties, his twenty-five-year military career, and twenty years at a chemical plant after retiring from the army. He discussed his traveling adventures, transport van, and medical equipment business with his brother, Moses, and his future goals. He even admitted that he had been married three times. "I believe in the institution of marriage and don't believe in shacking up."

He chatted with the server when he brought food to our table. We were so enthralled in each other's conversation that we didn't leave after dinner. Scotty tipped the waiter twenty-five percent, and we walked to the lounge area, found a cozy sofa near a fireplace, sat down, talked, and sipped white wine for nearly two hours.

While I enjoyed the aroma of his musk and smoky wood-scented cologne, Scotty looked at his watch and exclaimed, "Do you know it's nearly midnight? I've got to get up for church tomorrow morning, so we better get going."

Our eyes met, and I said, "I have to get up for church also."

He escorted me to my car, opened the door for me, held it until I had sat down behind the steering wheel, closed it, and shouted for me to lock my doors and be careful driving home. When I glanced in my rearview mirror driving away, he leaned on his cane as he watched my vehicle exit the parking structure and turn onto the main street.

Chapter Six

CHRISTMAS SURPRISE

Sunday night, I called to thank Scotty for dinner and told him I had a wonderful time. He asked if I trusted him enough to give him my telephone number. I had called the previous three conversations.

I breathed into the phone and smiled. "You don't seem like a stalker, harasser, or someone who will call and wake me at two in the morning. Sure, you can have my number. I enjoy talking to you."

He replied in a gravelly tone, "I don't want to talk to anyone that doesn't want to talk to me. Anytime you feel I'm harassing you, just let me know, and I'll stop calling."

My mouth gaped, and I hesitated before speaking. *Don't make a mountain out of a molehill. He's just being honest.* "That sounds fair to me." I gave him my home phone number only.

We didn't talk for hours as previously. Scotty said, "I need to pick up my daughter, so I'll call you later."

Around 9:00 p.m., he called and said, "Good night," and we hung up the phones.

After getting my phone number, he called every evening to say good night. Sometimes, we talked for an hour, but if I was tired or busy doing something, he would say, "I just called to say good night," and hang up.

The thoughts of him being much older flew away, and I looked at the character traits he presented: considerate, intelligent, and a churchgoing man. It was thoughtful of him to think about me every night and take the time to call to say good night.

Scotty invited me to his daughter's house for Thanksgiving, but I refused because I was hosting my family's Thanksgiving. When Christmas rolled around, we only knew each other for two months and agreed not to exchange gifts. On Christmas Eve, he called and asked if I wanted to go for a coffee.

"I'm sorry," I hesitated, deciding whether to halt my meal preparation and go for coffee or continue cooking. "I'm in the middle of preparing Christmas dinner."

He blew into the phone and said nothing.

I rubbed the back of my neck. "I would love to go for coffee, but I have cornbread in the oven, turnip greens on top of the stove, and am mixing my sweet potato pies."

He cleared his throat. "Sorry? I haven't seen you in a week." His voice lowered. "Can I come over? I can be there in fifteen minutes."

"I am not a good multi-tasker when cooking, and I need to focus on what I'm doing." I inhaled.

He whined. "You're going to be with your family on Christmas, and I'll be with Charlessa, and we won't see each other at all during the holidays."

There was quietness at my end.

He chuckled. "I won't get in your way and may be able to help...like peeling potatoes for potato salad." Before I could reply, he added, "I can wash dishes while you cook. You won't even know I'm there."

My head shook, but I finally said, "Okay, but I will not be a good host because I won't be able to entertain you."

"No problem," he quickly said before I changed my mind. "I'll see you in about fifteen minutes."

He arrived precisely fifteen minutes later and rang the doorbell, smiling, with a large white box in his hand when I peered through the stained-glass window at the top of the door. After I opened the door and invited him in, he leaned over and kissed my cheek.

My head tilted, and my lips twisted. "What's in the box?"

He ignored my question, took his brown leather jacket off, and threw it across the chaise. Figuring he would tell me when he felt like it, I returned to the kitchen and checked on my cornbread dressing.

"Do you have any eggnog?" He rubbed his hands together and licked his lips like I was bringing his favorite dish.

"No, I don't have any eggnog. I have juice, milk, and water. Do you want juice, milk, or water?"

Scotty shook his head from side to side. "Naw, I'm fine."

"I might have some leftover red wine. Let me check." I searched the fridge. "No. It's all gone."

He moved around in the kitchen and stared at me with a slight grin.

"How was your day? Have you wrapped all of your gifts?" I asked.

"Most of them; I only have one child, remember? But I have gifts for my sisters."

"Are you going to one of your siblings for Christmas dinner or just you and Charlessa?"

The questions prompted him to spend an hour telling me about his family's Christmas gathering, how they spent their Christmas, and that he usually did not attend any family gatherings. He told me whose house each sibling visited, how they exchanged gifts and explained in detail how he wraps his gifts differently from most people.

He leaned on the kitchen counter and folded his arms. "Today was spent shopping with Charlessa and thinking about you." His eyes widened, and his lips smiled. "I think about you all the time."

My face reddened, and I gazed toward the floor.

After strolling into the living room, he opened the large box and pulled out a white, floor-length mink coat. "Merry Christmas, sweetheart."

I gasped and threw my hands over my mouth.

He walked to me, wrapped the coat over my shoulders, and kissed my lips.

With wide eyes and raised eyebrows, I froze in my spot. We had decided not to exchange gifts, and I didn't have a present for him. I inhaled the animal aroma and rubbed my hands across the soft fur. "I can't accept this gift," flew out of my mouth in a tone more high-pitched than I intended.

A gift of a mink coat is too expensive to give to someone you've only known for two months, I thought. I shoved the garment from my shoulders and laid it on Scotty's arms. "I appreciate the gift, I really do, but we said we were not exchanging gifts this year, and I can't accept this one."

Still smiling, he asked, "Why not?"

"It's too expensive." My eyes went to the coat, and I hummed a sigh.

"Don't worry if you didn't get me anything." He lifted his head and pushed his chest out.

I mumbled, "We said we wouldn't exchange gifts this year."

"I know, but I wanted to do this for you. You deserve it, and you're worth it."

"What do you mean, 'I deserve it, and I'm worth it?'"

His eyes brightened, and his smile widened. "You carry yourself like a lady and are a jewel I've found."

My heart melted. I stood taller and clasped my hands behind my back. "Thank you for the gift. It's beautiful, but I can't accept it."

Scotty scowled, furrowed his brows, and said, "Don't make a big issue out of it! I wanted to buy this for you. It's my money, and I can do what I want with my own money."

A churning sigh slipped through my mouth before pressing my lips together. I said nothing while taking the cornbread dressing out of the oven. Finally, I said, "Take the coat home with you, and we can discuss it after Christmas."

"Fine." Scotty turned his shoulder away from me.

For about ten minutes, neither said anything, and then he said, "You don't know how to accept a gift without thinking strings are attached." He tossed the coat into the box.

"I never said anything about strings being attached." My arms crossed my body. "I said it was too expensive, and we both decided we would not exchange gifts."

"Yeah, yeah." The veins throbbed in his neck as his jaw clenched. "I don't want anything from you but your love."

My eyes darted sideways in his direction, and I returned to dicing vegetables for my potato salad. I turned the kitchen TV to a lifetime movie, trying not to let his behavior intimidate me. After watching a few scenes, I said, "Wow! That boyfriend is really controlling and manipulative. I'm glad we don't have to worry about those problems as we get better acquainted."

Scotty grunted and turned his back to the television. He stood in the kitchen for another five minutes without talking, finally saying, "I guess I'll head home," slipping his arms into his jacket.

"Okay, I enjoyed your visit." I wiped my hands on my apron, walked him to the door, and kissed his cheek. "I appreciate your thoughtfulness in buying me the mink," not noticing he didn't have the large box in his hand.

"Merry Christmas," said Scotty, pecking my lips. "I'll call you tomorrow."

"Merry Christmas to you and enjoy your family."

His head jerked toward me. "I won't be seeing my family."

I offered a forced smile, waved as he drove away, locked the door, and returned to the kitchen to finish preparing my Christmas dinner.

After frosting a chocolate cake, taking the turkey out of the oven, and covering the candy yams, I headed toward the main bedroom. Remembering to put on the night light, I strolled back into the living room and saw the large white box on the chaise. Scotty had left the coat after I asked him to take it with him.

Multiple thoughts flowed through my head. *I don't want him trying to buy me with a mink coat, and I don't want him to think I'm committing to a relationship if I accept the gift. Does he have that type of money? We didn't discuss his investments or pension income. Scotty was right when he said it's his money, and he can do what he wants with his money.*

I shook my head as more thoughts fluttered. *He shared that he enjoyed life traveling, attending sports events, concerts, and the theater. During one of our conversations, it slipped that he had not saved a dime and spent his money on pleasures, so how could he have this type of money? Did he say he didn't have a dime to see if I would stop going with him?*

I didn't know what to think, and it did not make sense. After thinking for quite a while and not reaching a conclusion about Scotty, sweating and puffing from Christmas preparations, I said, "I'll worry about it tomorrow. I'm too tired to think straight now. Maybe I *am* making too big of a deal out of it."

The phone startled me when it buzzed. "Hello," I said in a singsong tone.

"I just called to say good night," Scotty whispered.

"Good night," I replied, deciding to wait until after the holidays to discuss the gift.

We didn't see each other during the Christmas and New Year's holidays, but Scotty called like clockwork every evening to say good night.

It was mid-January before I convinced him to return the coat to the furrier. He frowned and said, "I'm disappointed you didn't just accept the coat as a gift instead of making a big production out of it."

My lips pressed together, and I blew air into my cheeks without responding.

Chapter Seven

TRUE COLORS SHOW

The next day, when he phoned, Scotty's voice was low and toneless. "Hello, how are you doing? How was your day?"

In his greetings before Christmas, he'd said, "Good evening. And how is my sweetheart this evening?" before starting a conversation.

As soon as "My day was okay" came out of my mouth, Scotty started ranting and complaining about me not keeping the coat as a Christmas gift. "I didn't think you were that selfish and inconsiderate of other people's feelings. I wanted to give you the coat; it should have been my decision. I'm beginning to see some things I don't like about you. You're very insecure. Do you know that?" He paused for effect. "You do know that don't you?" He then rattled for a full hour about how surprised he was to discover I was so selfish and uncaring compared to his being compassionate, selfless, and considerate.

When he took a deep breath, I said, "Scotty, I explained to you why
—"

He talked over me in a strident, breathy tone. "You hurt my feelings." He gasped for breath between sentences. "You didn't say it directly, but I noticed you were saying I was controlling when you said we decided not to exchange gifts, and I bought a gift anyway."

My heart rate galloped, pounding against my chest like a caged animal desperate to escape as I tried multiple times to interject. I inhaled and exhaled before finally sitting on my sofa, waiting for him to finish talking.

After he had said everything he could to offend me, he said in a soft-spoken voice, "When I care for someone, I show it, unlike you! You talk like my daughter and sisters; they say I'm too controlling. I'm a caring person, and sometimes I do become overprotective. Well, when I love, I love hard. When I care, I care deeply. I'll admit I'm overprotective, but I am not controlling." His tone became dead and emotionless when he said, "The hell with all of you!"

My mouth gaped, and my pulse sped up more. I stared at the phone with wide eyes. Scotty's tone softened before I could decide if I should hang up and call him back in a couple of days.

He acted like the first hour of the verbal attack had never happened. "So, what type of day did my sweetheart have today?"

He didn't give me a chance to respond.

He proceeded to tell me about his day. "I looked into some part-time job offers, but I'm still unsure if I want to work for someone else. Dealing with Medicare is a big enough headache. Most of our sales for our medical equipment are to companies that accept Medicare payments."

He chatted on and on in a singsong voice, laughing and discussing current events as though everything was as usual, and he had not just chewed me up and spat me out. He seemed unaware that he had verbally abused and demeaned me for sixty minutes.

My head heard him speaking, but my mind did not comprehend. His words echoed in my eardrums, twirling around in my head but not computing. I was still filtering his statement, "I'm beginning to see some things about you that I don't like," and trying to decipher why he went into the tirade and pointed out that he was not controlling, just overprotective. He didn't allow me to say one word, so why would he say I talked like his daughter and sisters?

Suddenly, a bulb went off in my head. While watching a lifetime movie on Christmas Eve, I said the boyfriend was controlling and manipulative.

Scotty had mulled over the conversation for a month and incorrectly assumed that I was hinting at him and decided this was the time to let me know how he felt.

As my mind rolled the negative comments through my head, Scotty yakked on and on, laughing at his jokes and not noticing that I was not contributing to the conversation. *What did he mean? I'm beginning to see things I don't like about you. Did he mean everything he said, or was he just venting frustrations? Would he listen now if I tried to give my opinions? Was it worth my getting upset about? He had a right to his feelings and thoughts. We were not in a serious relationship, and I could always tell him to stop calling me.*

His loud voice startled me when he called my name. "Hannah! I asked, what are your plans for tomorrow?"

A whisper came from my lips. "Nothing special, same old, same old."

"I have a couple of board meetings and may investigate the part-time gig one of the board members is encouraging me to take."

We said good night and hung up the phones. I reflected on the conversation for a moment and then shrugged my shoulders. I thought about our relationship. *I have been talking to Scotty every night since October. Is this the work of God, or do I just want companionship? I like talking to him, and it feels good to have a male friend who's interested in me and doesn't want to hang up when we're talking. But what are my feelings? Am I dating him out of desperation that I won't meet anyone else? Do I genuinely care for him, or is he just someone to spend time with?*

His outburst tonight scared me and brought back memories of my first husband's shouting and calling me nasty names. I do not want to get involved in another toxic relationship. Perhaps Scotty had a bad today and is just a little stressed.

I didn't know it then, but I discovered later in our relationship that Scotty didn't want to hang up because he felt that as long as he talked to me, he knew what I was doing and if I was with someone else.

After the bizarre conversation in January, Scotty was like a sweet angel. However, during Saturday morning breakfast that same week, out of the blue, he made a peculiar comment, "You can't be that perfect. I've tried to find something wrong with you, and I can't. You're smart, you're beautiful, you're a hard worker, you're ambitious, and you're a good mother. You seem to do everything right."

Why would he be trying to find something wrong with me? My initial reaction was to remind him of all the negative things he had said over the phone, but I decided against it. That's water under the bridge. Don't bring up old garbage, I thought. I said instead, "We're in the honeymoon phase of our relationship now, Scotty; you have blinders on. I'm a long way from being perfect. I'm a good person but not perfect by a long shot."

Scotty furrowed his brows, deepened his voice, and said, "I don't believe in that crap! What you see is what you get with me. So, you're saying you're pretending, and this is not how you are?"

My face tightened, and a scowl came. "No, that is not what I'm saying. I'm saying, Scotty, that people put on their best behavior when trying to impress each other at the beginning of a relationship. You won't let someone you like and are trying to impress see all of your negatives at the beginning."

Scotty's mouth twisted, and his nose wrinkled. "That's bull! You should be yourself all the time. There's no such thing as a honeymoon phase." He smacked the table. "It shouldn't make any difference if you just met the person or have known them for years; you should be the same person."

My body jumped when he hit the table, and I hoped he hadn't noticed. I worked hard to maintain my composure while I attempted to help him understand what I was saying with a few more statements, but his defenses were up, and he had stopped listening to anything I said.

After a while, he grunted and said, "I still say there is no such thing as a honeymoon phase."

A headache came, and I knew my subconscious was warning me. But I ignored the headaches and stress-eating whenever Scotty's controlling, judgmental, dominating, know-it-all behaviors poked holes into my spirit. The logical part of my brain rationalized that none are perfect, all humans have positive and negative traits, and that Scotty's positive attributes far outweighed his negative ones.

Because of his selflessness and consideration, like peeping through his blinds or standing in the yard until I was safely in the apartment when I visited, I ignored his obvious dysfunctional traits of insecurity and *dry drunk syndrome* behaviors. And I got entangled in his web and bedeviled into moving deeper into the relationship.

It started raining as we headed out of the restaurant. Scotty put his arm in front of my body. "Stay here, and I'll get the car and an umbrella."

"Just pull up to the door, and I can run to the car. You don't need to bring an umbrella." While I waited, I thought. *This treatment is what made me endure him.* A huge grin filled my face. *He even cleans the snow off of my car before I go to work.*

When we met for breakfast, he brought flowers, sometimes a single rose, carnation, lily, orchid; other times, he got two dozen roses. I guess it depended on how he felt that day or how much he wanted to impress me.

After the berating, he also began surprising me with gifts of clothing and jewelry, saying he was always thinking about me and that if he spotted something he thought would look good on me, he bought it. He had good taste in women's clothing and brought the cutest items, albeit longer and more oversized than I would have purchased for myself.

Thoughts surfaced that Scotty was not a genuine Christian but a churchgoing, Bible-carrying man. He attended church weekly and carried his Bible but rarely read it. During our discussions, Scotty said the Bible stories sounded like fables. I tried convincing him they were true stories, and he'd quipped, "Were you there? If you weren't there, you don't know if they happened."

After church on Sundays, he'd phone to complain about his church service, how wrong the pastor was in his message, the pastor's wife tried to take over the service, the praise and worship team sang too long, and the service should end in two hours instead of three to four hours.

I felt he had a right to his opinion, would give my understanding of church service, what I thought was the purpose of the sermon, that I felt the pastor's wife had a right to speak if her husband allowed, and that praise and worship could be as long as the Holy Spirit desired. After each discussion, he disagreed and said, "My grandfather founded the church and didn't hold long services like that. But I'm not going anywhere. I'll be there until I die."

Chapter Eight

OVERLOOKING OBVIOUS SIGNS

For Valentine's Day in 1998, Michelle hosted a dinner party, and the ladies separated into the living room after dinner. Scotty, Perry, Michelle's husband, and Markus, Shirley's spouse, stayed in the kitchen, drinking beer and watching basketball.

After hours of hearing Scotty dominate the conversation and disagree with everything Perry and Markus said, Michelle asked, "How do you and Scotty communicate? He hasn't stopped talking since we left the kitchen, and you haven't stopped talking since we entered the living room. When do you two listen to each other?" She locked eyes with me. "Seriously, Hannah, what type of communication do you two have? I haven't heard Markus or Perry say much since we left the kitchen, and when they start talking, Scotty interrupts them and takes over the conversation."

My face reddened, and I lowered my head. "Scotty doesn't think he talks that much." I gazed at both ladies. "He thinks that he's quiet and an excellent listener."

Michelle's eyes widened, "You've got to be kidding."

Michelle and Shirley started laughing loudly and holding their stomachs. Neither could believe that Scotty actually thought he didn't talk that much.

The men rushed to the living room to see what was so funny. Perry asked, "What's going on in here? What's so funny?"

Markus stood next to Perry, silent but smiling. Scotty hovered behind Perry and Markus, leaning on his cane, staring at the three of us, scowling, looking as though we three had had nervous breakdowns.

Shirley glanced at my taut facial expression and said, "We were talking about some of the odd people we used to work with and some of the funny things they did."

The tight facial lines on my face diminished, and I appreciated Shirley's quick thinking. I have no idea how Scotty would have reacted if he thought the ladies were laughing at him.

Perry and Markus smiled, nodded, turned, and returned to the kitchen. Scotty stepped back to the side of the doorway, leaning on his cane, glared at us again, frowned, and limped back into the kitchen. Driving home, he asked, "What were you girls talking about, and what was so funny that you all sounded like a pack of hyenas?"

In a quiet voice, I said, "Shirley told you what we were laughing about."

He glanced at me sideways, mumbled something under his breath, and drove the rest of the distance to my house in silence.

I tell you the truth; Scotty dominated the conversation wherever we went, yet said he was quiet and didn't talk that much. Multiple times, at functions with people he and I had just met, he dominated the conversation, talking about all of his surgeries, the medications he was on, his military adventures, his knowledge of hazmat protocols, or the places he had traveled.

Scotty was the expert on everything; in every discussion, whatever direction the conversation flowed, Scotty dominated it. When he spoke, he talked confidently about politics, economics, religion, travel, operating a successful business, facilitating a board meeting, raising children, everything, I tell you, everything!

I must admit that he was knowledgeable but not an expert on everything as he thought. Those characteristics drew me to him at the beginning of our courtship, but they became exasperating and blistering over time.

Scotty honestly believed that he didn't talk much, was an excellent listener, and wouldn't listen to me or anyone who tried to tell him he didn't listen and dominated conversations. Not receptive to feedback, he wouldn't receive constructive criticism at all. One day, a relative told him, "Man, you don't listen and think you know everything about everything."

Scotty retorted, "I'm not always right, but I'm never wrong."

One Saturday morning, while he and I ate breakfast, he started discussing current events. I corrected him on some incorrect data, and he continued to say the same inaccurate statements. After hearing him state the incorrect data several times, I rolled my eyes, shook my head, and said, "Scotty, you're not the expert on every topic. You can be wrong sometimes, too."

He repeated the phrase he'd said to his cousin, "I may not always be right, but I'm never wrong. I never talk about a subject if I don't know what I'm talking about."

It was such a ludicrous statement that I shook my head from side to side and said, "I give up!"

He based his conclusions of situations on his observing interactions between people. Once he decided that something was going on, he never changed it. No matter the facts demonstrated, he never recanted a decision or conclusion determined by him. When I'd say that everything is not black and white and has gray areas, he'd said, "All situations are either black or white; there is no gray area. It's good or bad, right or wrong."

Chapter Nine

REAL OR FAKE

When Easter rolled around, he invited me to his church, and I accepted. Scotty was the perfect gentleman; he strolled to my door, leaning on his cane, and rang my doorbell. Having learned during my conversations with him that he hated it when people were not ready when he picked them up, dressed and ready to go, I sat near the door. He'd told me stories of leaving his sisters in other states if they weren't in the car when he said he was going.

He said, "It's rude, selfish, and inconsiderate of people not to be punctual when someone else is driving." He habitually arrived at events one hour before the activity commenced.

After I stepped through the doors, he escorted me to a green, two-toned Lincoln Continental. An eyebrow lifted when I spotted the new vehicle; he hadn't told me about it during our conversations. We strode to the car, and he opened the door for me. After he slid behind the steering wheel, I said, "This is a beautiful car. You didn't tell me you had bought a new automobile."

"I don't have to report everything to you, do I?"

My voice stammered, "I'm just complimenting you on your good taste."

He smiled and winked at me. "Charlessa thought I needed a more modern car since I'm dating a younger lady."

We chatted about Charlessa until we arrived at the sanctuary and went inside. The parishioners were friendly, welcoming, animated, and vibrant while praising the Lord. I had a wonderful spiritual time at his church, but Scotty sat stone-faced in the chair next to me, his arms crossed and his eyes closed during most of the service. I nudged him periodically to check if he was awake.

After service, he grinned and stuck his chest out while introducing me to his pastor and some of the members. While driving home, he said, "It made me proud to have you accompany me today, and I am happy you went with me."

I returned the smile. "I enjoyed myself and may start coming to your service after mine ends since yours don't start until noon."

Scotty replied, "I would love that." He was silent for several moments and suddenly asked, "Will you marry me?"

A loud gasp came from my lips because of surprise, and my hands flew over my mouth. "Let's get to know each other better," I said, smiling.

"I love you. But I don't want to rush you, so I'll wait until you make up your mind."

After that, when my 10:00 a.m. service ended at my home church, I rushed to Scotty's church. Scotty napped during most of the service or limped in and out of the building five to six times. I figured he didn't smoke, so he only walked so much to stay awake. I wondered how he complained about the service when he rarely participated.

After attending Easter service, Saturday morning breakfast and Sunday dinner became a ritual. Most of the time, we went to one of the fancy restaurants that he liked. But, sometimes, I would prepare a traditional Sunday dinner on Saturday, and we would return to my home for dinner.

Since our first date in October, I had not dated anyone else, and Scotty and I spent more and more of our weekends together. He always had something planned for the weekends, purchased tickets to an event, concert, or festival, or made reservations for dinner. When dog-tired, I couldn't force myself to say no since he had already purchased tickets or made reservations and had broad grins on his face.

Chapter Ten

LUDICROUS THINKING

The First weekend in May, Shirley and Markus invited former co-workers to a barbeque at their home. On the drive to the cookout, Scotty yelled and criticized me because I wasn't dressed when he rang my doorbell.

I blinked away tears. Trying to vent my feelings and describe how Scotty made me feel, I said, "You talk to me like I'm a child. I'm trying to explain why I wasn't dressed."

He talked louder and more forcefully. "There is no excuse for not being ready when someone picks you up."

I raised my voice louder. "I'm hurt by all the negative things you said."

He lifted his voice several decibels. "I had such high regard for you when we first met. But now I see that you're just like the other women."

When he stopped talking to breathe, I defended myself, but as soon as he exhaled, he over-talked me again.

The next time he exhaled, I made several comments but mostly listened to him berate and degrade me to Shirley's house, wiping tears from my cheeks.

A thought flashed: why don't you role model how a good listener responds, hoping he would take notes? *I don't have to be discourteous because he's disrespectful and inconsiderate.* I told myself that if we were talking simultaneously, neither would hear what the other said. So, I gazed in his direction and nodded now and then.

Hurt by the verbal rebuking, speaking to me as if I was his child, and not listening when I tried to explain, I jumped out of the automobile as soon as we reached the house. I moved ahead of Scotty as he limped behind with his cane. When I entered the backyard, forcing back more tears trying to rain down my face, I ignored him and found a table for u
s.

Many colleagues I had worked with for ten years, hit clubs and concerts multiple times with, and had not seen for numerous years approached my bench. We gave cheek-to-cheek kisses, wrapped our arms around each other, and grinned like laughing Llamas.

At rare times, Scotty could be stand-offish and wouldn't talk to people he didn't like, eyeing them with tight lips. He was in one of those moods. After spotting me in the backyard, Scotty limped to the picnic table, where I chatted with friends. He sat under a brightly colored umbrella and crossed his legs and arms. As I talked with my former work associates, chills moved through my bones as Scotty glared.

Because I now realized that he scrutinized my conversations, actions, and reactions, I didn't go out of my way to talk to anyone unless they came to me. His non-smiling face, arms folded across his chest, one leg on top of his knee, glowered and watched me like a snake watching a rat. By then, I knew he studied everything I did or did not do, trying to catch me in a lie, as he later told me.

After several minutes, I moved into a chair at the head of the table next to Scotty. Scotty scowled and shifted to the opposite end of the bench without saying a word. Women and men strolled to our table, hugged and kissed me, and asked, "How have you been? What have you been up to? Where are you working now?"

I asked them the same questions, and we caught up with what had happened in our lives for the last ten years. My associates and I discussed our children, families, and places of employment. They congratulated me on stepping out and starting a business, and I became so immersed in the conversations that I forgot to introduce Scotty as my boyfriend.

With the space between me and Scotty's chairs, friends didn't realize Scotty and I were together, and other guests sat on the chairs between us. A male friend, Lenny Woodson, strode up to me, kissed me on the cheek, and said, "Hi."

We worked in the same office, spent much time on projects, and became close friends. We had lots of catching up to do, and we talked about our new jobs, children, and his relationship with Adelai. Lenny told funny stories and made boring topics enjoyable. We laughed and talked for quite a while about our old boss, making eye contact as one does when communicating. He pointed to Adelai, and I stood, smiled, and waved at her. I sat back down as Lenny headed in his girlfriend's direction, crossing my legs, still gazing toward Lenny and Adelai.

Most of the evening, old friends strolled to my area to chat, and with Scotty sitting at the opposite end of the table, it slipped my mind to introduce him. Perhaps it was subliminal or Freudian. But most men would have talked about how rude it was not to present your boyfriend and let it go. Not Scotty.

His eyes picked up what wasn't there, and his mind cooked up the fanatical conclusion that because I didn't introduce Lenny to him, talked to Lenny longer than any of the others, and "crossed my legs" after talking to Lenny, I was having an affair with him.

I couldn't believe it. Because I crossed my legs, I was having an affair. This crazy illusion continued with Scotty through our courtship, engagement, and marriage. After telling Scotty several times that Lenny was Adelai's boyfriend of ten years, one evening, he said, "Your friend, Adelai, is just a front for your affair."

I couldn't believe my ears. *Where did that thought come from?* My hands went over my mouth, and I stepped back and stared at Scotty, speechless.

Ludicrous. Ludicrous. Ludicrous. It was not logical, as Dr. Spock would say. Lenny and I were both single. Why would we need someone to front for us? Anger overtook the shock, and veins throbbed in my neck as I clenched my teeth to keep from saying the words going through my head.

Chapter Eleven

IRRATIONAL BEHAVIORS

Sensing Scotty's jealousy growing like an inflated exercise ball, I phoned Adelai to give her a heads-up. "Scotty has conjured in his head that I'm having an affair with Lenny."

Adelai burst out laughing. "You've got to be kidding. Didn't he see us together at the party?"

"I, I think so." I sighed, and my voice cracked. "He thinks you are a front for Lenny and me."

"That man is crazy. You need to get out of that relationship, Hannah."

I exhaled before speaking. "Scotty has some good qualities. He's protective, giving, and self-confident, and treats his daughter and sisters well. Yeah, he's jealous...." My shoulders shrugged. "But I think that will get better."

Adelai grunted. "I don't think so. You're seeing what you want to see and not what everyone else sees in him."

"I think you all just look for the negative in him because he out-talks everyone."

Adelai laughed. "We agree with that fact."

I couldn't stop myself from chuckling when I thought of Scotty's domination of the conversation with Markus and Perry. "Tell Lenny Scotty is very jealous and doesn't like men hugging or kissing me, even on the cheeks. He doesn't want Lenny to hug or kiss me anymore, and I'm trying to respect his wishes."

"I don't believe you're going along with that!"

"Scotty is older and thinks differently from our generation. When he grew up, men didn't touch other men's women unless something was happening between them."

"That's bull, and you know it, Hannah!"

An exasperated sigh slipped. "Let Lenny know so I don't have to deal with Scotty's attitude, okay?"

"Sure. If that's what you want. Are you all coming to the dance Saturday?"

"Yes, we'll be there."

On Saturday, when we arrived at the dance, Lenny and Adelai strode to my table and hugged and kissed me. My eyes quickly darted toward Scotty, and I whispered to Lenny, "Didn't Adelai tell you what I said about Scotty thinking you and I are having an affair?"

"We thought you were joking," said Adelai, glancing at Lenny. They chuckled, and Lenny winked at me and said, "I'm going to have some fun with him."

"I'm serious, guys." I moaned and grimaced. "Every time we go to an event and a man hugs, touches, or kisses me on the cheek, Scotty's face reddens and grows dark, and we quarrel about the incident for the next two to three weeks."

Lenny put his arm around Adelai's waist, winked at her, still smiling, and said, "Okay, Hannah, we hear you."

We had been friends for ten years, and they knew my behavior—that I was friendly, fun, outgoing, confident, and, most importantly, independent. They could not believe the Hannah they had known for ten years would let a man dictate her behavior. It was difficult for them to accept that the woman they had worked, socialized, traveled with, and become close friends with would change her behavior because a boyfriend didn't like men hugging her.

Therefore, they didn't believe I was changing my character and doing what Scotty desired. The devil handcuffed my mind to Scotty's, and I began thinking as he thought.

As I reflect, I can't believe it either. After turning forty and pondering questions, perhaps I was going through a reflective phase in my life, and Satan slipped thoughts into my head as he did Eve.

Life questions emerged in my mind throughout the day. *Where is my life headed? What does the future hold for me? What do I want to be doing ten years from now? Do I want to be alone? Why don't I have a good husband? Is it something that I'm doing wrong? Am I too independent, aggressive, or overly confident?*

Without deliberately planning it, I began being more submissive as it related to Scotty, agreeing to his commands not to communicate with Lenny, wearing longer, looser clothing, and participating in fewer and fewer events with my friends.

Manipulations in my head convinced me that acquiescence was how to keep my man. I think I looked up the wrong definition of submissiveness. Submissiveness does not mean giving up your identity and individuality and being a doormat for someone else. I dug the hole and chose to fall in it, allowing Scotty to control me day after day so that I didn't know who Hannah was anymore. When I found the courage to disagree, he yelled, argued, and refused to listen.

The day after the dance, I telephoned Shirley, puffing and crying, and commenced talking as soon as she said hello. "Scotty and I had a big disagreement this morning over something as trivial as me getting a body massage from a professional. He said it is the same as walking naked in the park and letting anybody see my body." I sniffled and wiped my nose. "He said I don't have any respect for myself to let strangers rub all over me, acting as though he doesn't understand they are trained, professional people, skilled in giving massages, and are not interested in my body. I told him it is the same as when a gynecologist does pap smears or professional breast exams. He is so stubborn!"

Shirley laughed loudly on the other end of the phone as I ranted and raved, and after I stopped talking, she said, "That's the way older men are, Hannah. They think differently from younger men." She chuckled again and said, "Well, Hannah, I guess you won't be getting any more massages."

"He will not stop me from doing something I enjoy and doing what I need to do to relieve stress."

"We'll see," said Shirley. "What did he say to your gynecologist example?"

A deep sigh sounded. "The know-it-all Scotty said I was full of it and cursed." Another rant started flowing from my mouth, "I couldn't communicate what I was trying to say. He took everything I said out of context and made me sound foolish. The more examples I used, the worse our communication grew. It hurt and disappointed me because he wouldn't listen. We used to have open conversations. Now, he hears nothing I say."

Shirley continued laughing as I let off steam, and when the tea kettle stopped whistling, she said, "It'll be okay, Hannah, trust me."

"I hope so. Scotty can be so jealous and stubborn and yet do such sweet things like buying me a diamond tennis bracelet yesterday."

"That's probably his way of apologizing."

"You think so?"

"Yeah. Some men don't know how to say sorry but buy gifts to show remorse."

I exhaled. "Shirley, the massage issue is not the worst of it. Scotty believes I'm having an affair with Lenny."

She gasped. "I know you're joking, right, Hannah?"

"I wish I were. After the barbecue last week, we fought about Lenny. And the dance last night made it worse."

Chapter Twelve

CHARMED BY MANIPULATION

On the second Saturday in May, he took me to a high-end dress shop after our usual breakfast time to pick out my birthday present for the next day.

We had dated for several months, and I was beginning to feel like he was my boyfriend and comfortable accepting gifts from him. We had not verbally committed, but neither was seeing anyone else. So, I figured we were a couple.

Scotty took me to St. John's, an expensive and exclusive store in the suburbs. He was reeling me in like a bass hooked on a fishing line. He picked the outfits he liked, and the clothing had no price tags. When the clerk rang the suits and jewelry up, I noticed Scotty gasp and step back but quickly pulled himself together again. He pulled his shoulders back, lifted his chin, and searched his wallet for his charge card.

Thinking that the three outfits and jewelry were more than he wanted to spend, I whispered, "I can put one of the outfits back."

He rolled his eyes, said nothing, and slapped the card on the counter. After we were back in the car, he told me he took me to St. John's because he thought that's where I shopped, and I deserved royal treatment like a queen.

To this day, I still have no idea what he meant by "deserved." We hadn't slept together, so I couldn't be deserving of the outfits for services rendered. Possibly, I deserved it because I didn't argue with him; however, I voiced my opinions. Maybe I deserved it because I didn't disagree with him often and usually did whatever he wanted.

He picked out a beautiful black and gold knit suit, a black dress with rhinestones above the knee split and collar, and a two-piece lavender and white knit suit with matching earrings for all three outfits. No man had ever spent that much on me, nor had I spent that much on myself. As a teenager, I daydreamed of wearing expensive designer clothes that fit perfectly and looked rich and classy, but I never believed I'd ever be able to shop at one of the designer stores.

The following Saturday night, when I wore the black and gold suit, my eyes darted, and my breaths quickened when the people stared as the host escorted Scotty and me to a front table he had reserved for the jazz concert.

I don't usually make a grand entrance. Scotty knew how to enchant and live extravagantly. Our table was directly in front of the musicians, and after dinner, we went upstairs to hear another jazz quartet. I sucked my stomach in, stood taller, and strode with precise, firm movements like the Queen Scotty said I was. I felt confident. I felt beautiful. I felt rich. The suit fit like a glove and presented a look of class.

Men and women eyed me when I entered the downstairs lounge and the upstairs area, strutting with my chest out, tummy in, and chin lifted. We had fun meeting and talking to the quartet's members at the jazz club. As I strolled to meet him for brunch at Le Pfister's the following day, my eyes sparkled, and I hummed. Scotty had surprised me with another jazz group from Scotland performing during the brunch.

And that added icing to the cake, making my birthday celebration memorable.

While we ate and listened to the soothing music, I felt it was a relaxing time to put my feelings on the table since Scotty was in a charming, agreeable mood. I said, "I'm not committing to a sexual or a long-term relationship by accepting the birthday gift. I'm not seeing anyone else, but I want us to get to know each other better."

He grinned and licked his lips. "I'm just happy you're mature enough to accept the gift this time."

I responded with a close-lipped smile, knowing he always had the last word in our conversations.

As if a thought suddenly popped into his head, he said, "Have I asked you for sex or to commit to a sexual relationship? That's not even on my mind. It must be something on your mind."

An eyebrow raised, and I rose and strolled to the fruit bar. When I returned, Scotty tilted his head and narrowed his eyes. "Where did you park?"

"In the hotel structure." I took a bite of watermelon. "Me and my sister stayed here last night."

His head jerked, and he glared at me. "I dropped you off at home last night."

"I know." I smiled. "I had to pick up changing clothes."

His voice deepened, and he said gruffly, "Where is your sister now?"

"She didn't want to interrupt our time alone, so she went home."

He glanced around the room as if looking for someone. "I don't believe your sister was here with you." He stood and gazed around the room. "Did you have some dude with you last night after I spent all that money on you?"

My face reddened, and my eyes squinted. "I wouldn't have told you I spent the night here if I had been with another man." A distressed sigh dropped from my mouth. "I could have just told you my son dropped me off if I had a man waiting upstairs."

"I'm walking you to your room to make sure."

I rubbed the back of my neck and shook my head. "I'm checked out of the room, Scotty."

He stared without losing eye contact. And I stared back, my arms folded across my chest.

He bowed his head, stared at his plate for a while, then said, "Anywhere else you wanna go?"

"This has been the best birthday ever." I squeezed his hands between mine. "We missed church today, and I'm tired. Can you walk me to the structure?"

He scowled. "I don't know why you asked me that. I'm not going to let you walk alone."

Chapter Thirteen

DENYING UNREASONABLE ACTIONS

Shirley invited us to her son's graduation dinner at one of the downtown hotels on the third Saturday in May. Shirley, Markus, Michelle, Perry, Scotty, and I sat together while Lenny and Adelai disc-jockeyed behind a booth. As they strolled to our table, Lenny held Adelai's hand, him smiling and her giggling.

When they reached our table, Lenny strutted past everyone else, stepped to me, leaned over, and kissed me on the cheek from behind before I realized what he was doing. If looks could kill, Lenny would be dead in his grave from the cutting glare Scotty gave him. I was even shocked by Lenny's behavior since I had seriously explained to him and Adelai that Scotty didn't like men hugging or kissing me and that I was determined to make this relationship work, come hell or high w ater.

Frowning at Adelai and Lenny, I gazed at Scotty, and then my eyes darted to Lenny, "I asked you not to kiss or hug me, Lenny because Scotty doesn't like it."

Scotty glared into Lenny's eyes with clenched fists, a blackish-gray silhouette covering his face. He said in his most resounding bass voice, "That's right. I don't appreciate anyone else touching what belongs to me. If I had my knife, I would cut your throat."

Lenny chuckled, still not believing Scotty was serious. "I hear you, man. I won't do it again." His eyebrows waggled as he turned and said hello to everyone else at the table. He tapped my shoulder as he and Adelai strutted back to the disc jockey's booth.

Scotty grabbed the table to stand, but by the time he arose, Lenny and Adelai were playing music.

I exhaled, glancing sideways at Scotty, thinking the situation with Lenny was dead and buried. Scotty heard me tell Lenny not to hug or kiss me, and Lenny responded that he wouldn't do it again.

Scotty cursed a few times, staring in the direction of Lenny. He pouted through dinner, talking little, his eyeballs glowering toward the DJ's booth. Markus and Perry tried to get Scotty to relax and forget about the incident, telling him that Lenny likes to have fun and didn't mean anything.

My skin crawled, and my muscles jerked as I felt the evil spirits obtruding from Scotty. After long stares at Lenny, Scotty eventually enjoyed his meal and returned to his usual dominating character, changing Markus and Perry's discussion from sports to politics. He chatted with the four at our table but ignored me for the evening.

My face burned with embarrassment, but I attempted to stay poised and unaffected in front of my friends.

Before we entered the hotel's door, Scotty snarled, "You don't have any respect for yourself if you let anyone kiss and paw all over you. I thought you were a lady. You're not a lady; you're a slut! I thought you were better than that. I am so disgusted with you."

He spat on the ground. "I thought you handled yourself better than that, that you had respect for yourself. If you respected yourself, you should have stopped him from kissing you. I used to think you deserved to be treated like a lady, but I was wrong."

"I was shocked, just like you, when Lenny kissed my cheek."

He brushed me off and talked on and on and on about how disgusted he was with me. "You enjoyed it. I know you, and that coward got something going on."

"There is nothing between Lenny and me but friendship."

"You're a slut, and I am just disappointed because I thought I had found a lady. You're just like the women from the streets. I might as well have picked up a whore from the streets." He turned his shoulder away from me. "I would have been better off."

Instead of anger, shame came because I allowed him to talk to me that way. I covered my face with my hands, interjecting several times that Lenny leaned in and kissed me so quickly that I didn't have time to tell him to stop. Tears welled in my eyes. "I called him and Adelai last week and insisted he not kiss or hug me anymore. I didn't expect him to do it again."

Scotty had selective hearing and heard enough to respond. "That's what I mean. He doesn't have any respect for you if you told him not to hug or kiss you, and he groped all over you anyway." He glanced at me. "I went to prison for murder once and don't mind going again."

My hands went into the air. "What was I supposed to do, Scotty?"

He stared with wide eyes and a twisted mouth like I was a stranger. "Push him away or move away from him."

My head shook. "He did not touch me! He only kissed my cheek from behind." I sighed. "And I tilted my head when I realized what he was doing." Blinking back the tears, I decided it wasn't worth stressing myself out more, trying to explain to him that Lenny and Adelai didn't believe me and thought it comical for them to stop hugging and kissing me after ten years.

Then, it dawned on me what he'd said, *"I went to prison for murder once and don't mind going again." Was he serious or trying to scare me?*

The next day, a dozen red roses arrived from Scotty. No apology, but I assumed the flowers were his way of saying he was sorry for overreacting.

I didn't realize it, but Satan was using Scotty, his spiritual son, to try to steal, kill, and destroy my life. He was trying to ruin my relationship with my heavenly Father, Jesus, and the Holy Spirit, setting me up to steal my joy, destroy my peace, and kill my spirit. Before Scotty, I was friendly and gregarious, and Satan was hoping to kill that warm, outgoing spirit God had given me and replace it with fear, introversion, and depression.

Glory to God in the highest! Hallelujah! I was covered with the protecting and powerful blood of Jesus Christ and belonged to the family of God, so Satan could not touch or harm me. Even though he tried with limited power, Lucifer had no control over God's child unless I gave in totally to his cunnings and manipulations.

Understand me; Satan has authority. You've heard the names Satan, Devil, Lucifer, and Prince of Darkness, just a few of the names given to the angel thrown down from heaven when he lifted in pride and started thinking he was God. That took some nerve to imagine that you are as great as the one who created you. It was also foolish. But, when egotism lifts us, we do some stupid things.

Satan had it made in heaven, one of the top angels, an angel of beauty and power, but he messed it up when he became prideful. He had to leave the peace, serenity, protection, provision, and beauty of heaven. Of course, that old devil was enraged when Yahweh threw him out of heaven and determined to get back at Yahweh.

What do you think he did? Satan decided to compete with the all-powerful God for the children of the earth. It determined him to try to steal, kill, and destroy everything that belonged to God—the environment, communities, government, marriages, and especially human beings.

Doomed for eternal damnation, Lucifer wants to entangle as many of God's children as possible. His goal is to hurt God. He understands that God loves his creation and formed humankind like Himself, in His image.

Elohim desires that all humanity spend eternity with Him forever and ever after, transitioning from physical death to spiritual life.

The trickster, Satan, realizes that God gave humankind *free will*—the ability to decide freely. So Satan plays with our minds. He can only get to Jehovah's creation through our thought processes. The devil fills our minds with conflicting viewpoints and confusing thoughts, making the unreal appear natural, the immoral appear moral, the unlawful look lawful, and the unspiritual seem spiritual.

Lucifer creates aberrations and makes people see things that are not there, such as causing Scotty to see Lenny caressing me instead of giving me a cheek kiss.

Scotty visualized and heard some of the most unbelievable things and accused me of nonsensical things. One evening, while entering a video rental store, a man young enough to be my son held the door open for me, but Scotty saw him grinning and touching my hand.

Another time, accompanying Scotty when he applied for a loan, he accused me of whispering and flirting with the loan officer.

While searching for Tylenol in his medicine cabinet that night, I spotted a bottle of anti-depressant pills. I never noticed any signs of depression or abnormal behavior in Scotty, and I asked why he was taking mental health meds.

Surprisingly, he calmly stated, "That is not a psyche med. I take that for pain."

I accepted his reply because many medications are used for different purposes. After that discovery, I justified some of his erratic behavior as side effects of the many medications he ingested.

I believe he thought that he saw and heard those things because Satan created images in his head, and the incidents were as authentic to him as they were counterfeit to me.

My goal is not to glamorize Satan. As best as I can, I am describing how I met and married the man I felt was Satan's son because of Scotty's evilness and mean-spiritedness.

Why did I stay in the relationship?

I shrug my shoulders and say, "I thought that enough love, agreeing with him, ignoring other men when they spoke or smiled, and standing by my man, wrong or right, would make him trust me and realize I chose him, not the other men.

While going through hell, I initially believed I was dating Satan himself, but then I remembered I would not be on Earth anymore.

If I belonged to Lucifer, the covering of the blood of Jesus Christ would have departed, and Satan would have killed me quicker than a lightning flash. That's how little he cares about those who belong to him.

Chapter Fourteen

LONELINESS BLINDS YOU

In June, a few weeks after we celebrated my birthday, Scotty called my second shift job on Friday and asked, "What do you have a taste for this evening?"

"I don't know. I hadn't thought about it." I blew air into my cheeks.

Scotty chirped, "I'm cooking dinner for you this evening." He laughed into the receiver. "So, you can come over here when you get off work, and you don't have to go home and cook. What do you have a taste for?"

I thought for a moment. "Mmmm, baked salmon and a salad sound nice."

"Baked salmon and salad it is," said Scotty. "See you around 7:30."

"Okay, I'll see you around 7:30."

After hanging up, I hummed and smiled for most of my four-hour shift. Our first eight months had been a whirlwind—restaurants, theaters, concerts, festivals, and church. I had not met any of his relatives or been to his residence those eight months. He said his apartment was in the process of remodeling, or something was getting updated or repaired each time we planned to spend the evening at his place, and I was excited about seeing where he lived and spending time in his home.

When I arrived at his address, I was surprised to see he lived in low-income housing. I double-checked to ensure I was at the right place. Since Scotty walked with his spine straight and head high, wore expensive clothes, and took me to elegant restaurants, in my mind, I imagined he lived in a gorgeous, six-bedroom home or condo in the suburbs. Thoughts soared through my head of our past eight months, trying to grab anything I missed, showing he was a fake.

After parallel parking in a space directly in front of his unit, I sat in the car for several minutes, checking the surroundings and deciding if I wanted to get out. Thinking it would be uppity and impolite not to go in since I had told him I would be there, I unlocked my door. My pulse and breath sped up as I gazed around twice, and not spotting anyone approaching, I jumped out, speed-walked to the door, and rang the doorbell. He answered at the first ring, a broad smile on his face, wearing a chef's apron and cap.

Leaning on the screen door, he extended his hand toward the inside. "Come in and make yourself at home." He pecked my lips before I entered.

After entering the small area, I glanced around and didn't see a closet door. "Where should I hang my shawl?"

His tone was gravelly as he pointed, "In the closet; where else?"

"What closet?" I twisted my neck left and right.

"Look behind you, Hannah. Do you see that big brown door? Well, that's a closet. You can hang your wrap there unless you want me to hang it for you."

"No, no. I can hang it up. I didn't see that door. Sorry!"

He strode back into the kitchen as I hung my shawl on a hook. As I followed him, I went through the dining room. A white, lace, and satin tablecloth covered the table, and a bouquet of yellow roses in a crystal vase filled the middle. Orange and red flames flickered from the candles on two brass three-tiered candelabrums.

"This is beautiful, Scotty. You didn't have to go to all this trouble for me."

"It wasn't any trouble," Scotty responded. "Plus, you're worth it."

My voice caught in my throat. There, Scotty repeated that "You're worth it" phrase. Not wanting to ruin the evening that he had spent much time preparing for, I didn't question what he meant by "You're worth it."

We enjoyed a wonderful meal and had an enjoyable conversation without debating or disagreeing with each other, as had become habitual because Scotty felt his opinion was always correct. After washing dishes together, I prepared to leave since my day job started at 6:00 a.m.

"Why don't you spend the night?" He held my hand. "I promise I won't try anything and will sleep on the sofa." He gazed into my eyes. "You know I'm a man of my word. If I say I will do something, I do it."

My head shook. "I'd better head home."

"Do you need to take the dog out or something?"

A chuckle slipped from my mouth. "You know I don't have a dog."

"I'd feel safer if you stayed here since it's after 10:00."

He had a response for every reason I gave, and finally, I said, "I don't want to spend the night, Scotty. I want to go to my own house and my own bed."

He put his hands in his pockets and leaned back on his heels against the wall. "Why didn't you just say that at the beginning instead of making up all those excuses? That's all you had to say; you don't want to spend the night at my house."

At a loss for words, I grabbed my shawl out of the closet, wrapped it around my shoulders, pecked Scotty on the lips, thanked him for dinner, and headed to my car. After glancing around several times, he followed me to my vehicle and opened the door. "Lock your doors," he said as I slid behind the steering wheel. As I drove away, I glanced in my rearview mirror about a half block down the street, and he still stood on the porch staring in my direction.

The following Friday, he left a note on my car at my day shift job saying he had baked corn beef, fried cabbage, corn muffins, and plantains waiting when I ended my second shift at 7:00 p.m. After finishing my tour of duty at my business enterprise and working four hours at the school, I went to Scotty's.

By now, I was eating dinner with him every Friday and Sunday evening and meeting him for breakfast every Saturday morning. It started as a weekly Friday dinner gathering. He prepared dinner, and we read and discussed Bible passages. My eyebrows lifted when he asked basic questions about the scriptures, such as, "What do the red letters mean? What is the difference between the old and new Testaments?"

I expected him to be more mature in the scriptures because of his age. I ended up doing Bible teaching every Friday when we read together. Not entertaining the possibility that he did not know the Word of God; I attributed his lack of understanding to memory loss due to his age or the many medications he took.

By July, I was at his place eating my favorite entrée, vegetable, or dessert almost daily. He kept his refrigerator and cabinets stocked with my favorite foods.

Enjoying the time spent with a companion, I began looking forward to our Friday, Saturday, and Sunday outings.

While driving to meet him for breakfast, a seesaw of emotions went up and down in my head. One thought warned me to get away from Scotty's toxic grip. Another reflection encouraged me to cling to the love Scotty and I shared. I questioned whether I loved him or just liked the attention. *Scotty and I must be in love; we don't want to leave each other when we're together. But do I really love him, or is this my "stupid, passionate flesh craving attention?" This senseless, impious flesh of mine will lead me astray. I think I'm making more out of this relationship than I should. Geez, I'll enjoy the time with him, the attention he gives me, and wait for you, Lord, to show me why we're together and where the relationship is going.*

When I reached the restaurant, I concluded that destiny would take over.

Chapter Fifteen

LOOKING THROUGH CLOSED EYES

I convinced myself I was too picky and selective and would never meet a man who met my list's qualifications. Maybe Scotty was a blessing in disguise, and I needed to open my eyes to reality. Perhaps my prayer request was selfish.

Scotty had discussed marriage three months into the relationship, and I told him we needed to get to know each other better. During one of our Friday night Bible readings, he said, "After we're married, we can teach Sunday school together, run the food pantry, and do ministries as a couple."

A warm feeling had moved slowly through my body, and the thought of marrying him moved up several notches. I began convincing myself that Scotty was the husband I patiently and faithfully waited for.

He now had my mobile and three work site numbers. At this juncture, he mostly said the right things, did the right things and appeared to have morals and integrity.

I excused the incidences of jealousy and verbal abuse as him having a bad day or a generational thing because of his age. With Satan's help, Scotty even convinced me that his outbursts were typical because of his generation.

I forgot that Satan studies us from birth, learns our likes and dislikes, knows our weaknesses, and uses people to get to us through our frailty.

Lucifer knew I was praying for a husband and sent Scotty to block my genuine spouse from seeing me. Satan sends seeds of temptations, watches the fruit grow in us, and when our spirits are ripe for picking, he sends what we want, not what we need, to lure us into his kingdom.

The point I'm making is that Satan knew the desires of my heart. He knew that I wanted to feel special and desired a man to call nightly to say good night and sent Scotty to fulfill them.

Scotty was a charming, smooth operator with multiple tricks up his sleeves. During our first weeks of chatting over the phone, he listened more than he talked, discovering my likes, dislikes, weaknesses, favorite places, and favorite foods. When I started spending time at his apartment, he kept my favorite foods, fruits, vegetables, and desserts at his house.

As our tenth month approached, I imagined I had found "Mr. Right," although he did not meet the criteria I had listed.

Scotty presented himself as the perfect man—caring, unselfish, considerate, protective, and a provider – and one not pressuring me for sex. Since October, we had exclusively dated, seeing each other every weekend and talking every night.

Not talking to or contemplating dating anyone else, I found myself thinking about Scotty more each day.

During one evening of meditation, I wrote in my journal that I was waiting on God to move in my life, waiting on Jehovah to show me my husband, soul mate, and the man I was to spend the rest of my life with. I jotted in my journal. *I cannot choose for myself.*

Saying I could not choose was a mistake because God gives us free will, and me not making a decision was choosing. My staying in the relationship was my choice and my choice alone. The several times I broke up with him could have ended the drama, but time after time, I chose to give Scotty another try, bewitched by his promises and gifts.

Instead of fleeing from Scotty as a rabbit sprint from a fox, I put the responsibility on the Lord to choose my mate, saying, "Lord, you look at the heart and spirit, not just the flesh. You're better at picking than me. I've messed up so often with men that I'm scared to choose for myself."

Lucifer loved it when I said I was frightened, for he understands that faith cannot work if fear is present. The flesh is so deceptive that after I prayed, I thought I decided by the spirit when the flesh was in total control.

My spirit sincerely tried to pray and ask God's direction, vowing to turn it all over to my Father and do what He said. But I kept taking it back.

My confusion shows that Satan's deception and my lust trapped me, so I missed God's voice. Jehovah is not a God of confusion, which is what I had with Scotty twenty-four-seven. Experiencing and observing Scotty's hateful demeanor of mistrust, insecurity, quick temper, inability to forgive, and bitterness should have been a loud wake-up alarm.

He also held onto issues that made him vindictive, resentful, and dishonest.

But I disregarded the flashing signs and held onto Scotty as if he was the best thing since fast food restaurants.

Chapter Sixteen

CHRISTMAS DISAPPOINTMENT

The Holy Spirit showed me Scotty and I would never have an active life together. Scotty was sixty-five years old, with rheumatoid arthritis, high blood pressure, bad knees, back issues, bilateral hip replacements, and was taking multiple pills. I observed and experienced all of this. Yet, I stayed in the relationship.

Insanity!

Scotty had asked me to marry him several times, and in September, while at a street festival, he proposed again. "We were created for each other. I'm a good man and will be a good husband. I don't want your house or anything that belongs to you. I love you and want to marry you."

"I'll think about it," I'd replied, pressing my lips together.

When we celebrated our first anniversary in October, Scotty asked me again to marry him. "We can stay engaged as long as you want. Just say you'll marry me. I love you and think about you all the time."

I haven't noticed anyone else that interested me in the year we've been dating, and I can always break the engagement off as I did with my last two boyfriends. One shoulder lifted, and I said, "Okay, I'll marry you. I love you too."

When I said I'd marry him, a slight poking of unrest stirred in my spirit, but I shrugged it off. I loved Scotty and believed he was a decent man and would make a good husband, but I also knew that something was missing.

A bubbling and twisting started in my stomach whenever he suggested we look at rings. I had said yes to the proposal but was not excited as most brides are about picking the wedding bands, dress, venue, food, or cake.

I procrastinated with setting a date and selecting a ring, bouncing it off that the enthusiasm was missing because this was my second marriage, and I was busy building my Adult Family Home business.

As the manipulative and controlling person he was, Scotty called on Christmas Eve and told me to meet him at Sam's. We put multiple items in our cart, and then he led me to the jewelry section, found a ring that he liked, and asked, "What do you think? I can't afford the one we looked at in October. Money isn't coming in like it was then." He smirked. "You should have picked one, then. You could have gotten any ring that you liked."

It was a quarter-carat solitaire, and he seemed so excited about putting the ring on my finger that I ignored the thoughts in the back of my head, saying, "Something is just not right."

After Scotty slid the ring on my finger, I stared at the diamond as I twisted it around.

Scotty cleared his throat. "My charge cards are maxed out, and I need to pay them down." He sighed loudly, pressed his lips together, and said, "Is this ring not good enough for you?" His head tilted.

Attempting to be sensitive to his economic situation and less materialistic, I said, "Whatever ring you buy will be okay." That was my mistake because I was dishonest in not showing him the ring I wanted. This one was cute and what he said he could afford. I couldn't force myself to reject the engagement ring.

"Maybe I'll trade it for a bigger diamond before we're married."

A smile came, and I said, "Okay."

Therefore, he bought my engagement ring from Sam's Club.

Christmas rolled around, and excitement bubbled inside me, expecting the white mink coat he gave me our first Christmas together since we were now engaged. He gave such lovely gifts year-round that my body felt like it would explode in anticipation of my special Christmas gift.

After only knowing me for two months, he had given me a fur coat so I could not sit still, glancing through the blinds for Scotty's car and pacing through the house as I waited for him to ring my doorbell. When he arrived and handed me the white box, I was like a kid in a toy store. I snatched the wrappings off, opened it, and my smile faded when I spotted a black two-piece suit.

I forced a smile and held the Calvin Klein suit up, noticing the calf-length skirt first and then the larger size. "Thanks for the suit. It's beautiful but the wrong size." I kissed him on the cheek.

"What do you mean the wrong size? I know what size you wear." His head tilted as he stared at me.

I inspected the size again, which was bigger than what I wore. "You are good at picking out ladies' clothes."

"Women's clothes." He opened his gift and smiled broadly at the two new suits I had given him.

We ate Christmas dinner by candlelight, washed dishes, and played Scrabble until he became too obnoxious, challenging all the words I placed that I couldn't concentrate anymore. He challenged every word I thought of, and even when they were in the dictionary, he said, "That is not a word. Where did you get this dictionary? Those syllables should not be considered a word."

After getting a headache from scrabble, I feigned tiredness by yawning and stretching.

"How about I teach you chess?"

I had had enough for one night. "Perhaps, next time. My head hurts, and I'm ready to go to bed."

He lingered for another thirty minutes, put on his tan cashmere overcoat and matching cap, and kissed me. "I'll call you when I get home."

True to his word, my phone rang thirty minutes after he had left.

"Hello..." I said, with little emotion.

"I just called to say good night and tell you I love you."

"I love you too. Good night."

Chapter Seventeen

REJECTING THE HOLY SPIRIT'S WARNINGS

After securing the house, brushing my teeth, washing my face, and stepping into a tub of hot bubbles, I rested my head on a tub pillow, relaxing and enjoying the water's warmth and the eucalyptus smell, reflecting on the day's activities.

My lips mumbled, "Why would he give me such an expensive gift after only knowing me two months and give me a gift this year that looks like he didn't put any thought into it?"

I closed my eyes, took a deep breath, and reflected. *Scotty and I are like an old married couple; we eat breakfast together every week, attend church together, talk every night, and quarrel and fight like an old married couple tired of each other. The waitresses even ask us how long we've been married.* A still, small voice whispered, "What about the verbal abuse, the put-downs, the angry attacks, and the accusations? Do you want to be married to that character of a man?"

My head shook, and I said, as though talking to a friend, "No! I do not want to be married to a man like that."

"Then why did you accept the engagement ring?" said the same voice.

I glanced around as though someone was in the room with me. "I don't know." I continued conversing with the Holy Spirit, "Yes, Scotty is older than the mate I was expecting. But he's never raised his hands like he wanted to hit me, and I've fallen in love with him." I buried my face in the warm, soapy water.

However, I am concerned about the verbal attacks, jealousy, and constant accusations. I'm unsure if I'm doing the right thing by following my heart. Maybe I should also listen to what's coming from my head.

My chin rested on steeple fingers as I continued my reflections. *I desire many things missing in Scotty: romance, passion, holding hands, or massaging my shoulders. He doesn't like to show affection in public.*

I spoke into the atmosphere, "My husband will love, respect, honor, cherish, protect, and be thankful to God that he has found a good wife and treat me as his queen."

After stepping out of the tub, I threw on my white terry bathrobe and folded a quilt at the foot of the bed. I leaned against the headboard on four fluffy pillows. A low hum came from my throat, and I continued to talk to the Holy Spirit. "Scotty and I have been exclusively dating for over a year now. He's not pressuring me for sex and seems content having me as his companion. That's something to his credit."

I nodded as if answering a question. "I know. Scotty doesn't meet my 'compatibility requirements.'" I'd pay attention if I heard myself say some of my thoughts out loud. *I'm probably too picky, anyway.* "We like many of the same things, and at least I have a companion for the theater and dinner."

Am I fooling myself? Will I marry a man old enough to be my daddy?

"Yes, I will marry a disabled man twenty-five years older than me." As I reflected and spoke out loud, Satan listened. He knew my requirements for my husband, so all he had to do was make me see in Scotty what I wanted in a mate and not his actual character traits.

While my body shifted positions several times, my thoughts fluttered from breakfast that morning to my long, hot bath. Unable to fall asleep, I turned to my left side, then to my right, fluffed two pillows, and turned from left to right again, trying to force sleep. I switched to my stomach, back, right, and left, fluffed the pillows, and turned to my right side again, whispering a prayer. I jolted up and shrieked, "Why can't I fall asleep?" *Did anything significant happen to cause me to stress?* "No, nothing that I can think of."

The disappointment with the Christmas gift wasn't severe enough to cause stress. *I never have a problem falling asleep. When my head hits the pillows, I am dead to the world.*

Deep breathing exercises I practiced at my job crept through my head. I breathed in through my nose until my stomach was tight against my rib cage and blew out through my mouth, counting to ten. Sleep still wafted past.

My thoughts went back to marriage. *It would be nice to have a loving husband, someone to talk to at night when I can't fall asleep, and a smiling face to wake up to.*

Thoughts about my first husband and the men I had dated over the years slithered into my head. My thoughts settled on Scotty - the day's activities, past situations with him that drew tears, and his negative and positive qualities.

Past relationships that shattered my heart zigzagged through my mind like a maze. Sighing and resting my jaw on my hand, I snatched my journal from the bedside table. Journaling gave me clarity and helped me organize emotions when I wrote them down and reread them the next day.

The pen started writing about Scotty.

He is not an evil man. I believe he loves me. He is just too overprotective and jealous. He says he is not jealous; he just cares deeply.

I paused, stared into space for several seconds, and resumed writing.

He bought me a beautiful suede pantsuit for Valentine's Day with fur sleeves and a fur collar, so why am I disappointed because of the Christmas gift?

A heavy sigh slipped from my lips.

He never lets anyone say anything negative about me. A nervous chuckle slipped out as I rubbed my chin.

Granted, he says many negative things about me, but he defends me if others say something, like when his cousin challenged me on a statement I made about religion.

Another deep sigh tiptoed out.

His fatherly and protective nature causes him to step up when someone says anything about me or to me.

My fingers rested on the pen as I stopped writing, closed my eyes, meditated for a moment, and continued journaling.

Look how he stood up for me when we attended his uncle's funeral last month. His aunt wanted him to ride in the limo and said they only had room for one person. He demanded I ride with him, or he would not ride in the reserved vehicle.

I would have been driving in a strange city alone if he had not done that.

After wetting my lips, I sat straight up.

I think Scotty would make a fine husband. He's caring and protective. Scotty would be an excellent provider and can be sensitive when he chooses to be.

Thoughts about the incident months ago, when Adelai said Scotty tried to run Lenny off the road, slithered into my head. I didn't know who to believe. Scotty never actually denied doing it. Charlessa told me Scotty borrowed Moses's black Toyota SUV often. So he could have been driving the truck.

My shoulders hunched up and down. If the incident happened, I'm sure it was an accident, and Scotty did not purposely try to run Lenny off the road.

Charlessa also detailed Scotty's torrid pattern of abusive behavior towards her mother. This information should have reinforced that I needed to flee from Scotty's grasp. But I felt helpless and vulnerable to his charms.

My journal snapped shut, and I placed it and the pen back on the bedside table. "I love Scotty, and I am going to marry him. I need to trust him." My prayer that night was for God to show me what to do. I switched the lamp off, and a deep sleep finally arrested me.

As I drove to work the following day, I was more conscious of the couples as I glanced at the cars passing me. Everyone had a partner in the car but me. *Am I the only single female in the city of Madison?* Satan played with my head again, telling me everybody had a partner but me.

Emotions of sadness and loneliness swam through my body, and "you need a husband, you need a husband, you need a husband" banged inside my head. Every action starts in our mind first. The more we obsess and think about a person or something the flesh desires, the more enticing it becomes, and we begin thinking that we can't live without it.

When a couple in a red car passed on my right, I mouthed, "I'm waiting for my Father God to bring my husband and me together and to let my spouse and me know through the Holy Spirit it is our destiny to be husband and wife." I ignored that I had accepted Scotty's marriage proposal and did not realize Satan was sucking me deeper and deeper into his plan, and God was not in it.

My mouth whispered that I was waiting on God, but my head said you are alone, unloved, and the only one in your group not married. Self tried to handle the emotions instead of letting God keep control. I played right into Satan's hands and was determined to marry his spiritual son, Scotty.

As I look back, only weeks before meeting Scotty, I attended a women's conference and rededicated my life to God, genuinely seeking to get closer to Yahweh and do His will. Satan doesn't want that to happen, so he sent an intelligent, big spender to seduce me. I was set up and tumbled head-first into the devil's trap.

Satan hated me more when I faithfully attempted to practice Biblical truths, killing the fleshly desires and living holy. He, therefore, drew and enticed me with greater intensity, whispering half-truths and twisting my mind, his goal to destroy me by any means necessary. Lucifer is perpetually at his job, lurking around, seeking whom he can kill or destroy. Satan turns what is good into evil, honesty into dishonesty, and righteousness into evilness. He switches our sincere intentions into deceptive behaviors.

Lucifer was listening and lurking when I wrote in my journal and moaned about being the only single female in Madison.

The following night, Satan was listening when I prayed, "Lord, I thank you for giving me the gift of discernment and showing me how to follow the spirit, not my intellect. Thank you for showing me how to see Jesus and goodness in people, looking into their souls and spirits, and not judging others based on what I observe. Thank you for my mate. I do not want to age alone. Thanks for crucifying my selfish, stubborn, lazy, stupid body. I declare that my flesh is dead to any control by the devil, and the spirit of Jehovah reigns in my life."

The prayer words spewed from my lips but didn't embed in my heart, so Satan twisted my thoughts.

That old devil reinforced in my head that everyone had a mate but me, and if I didn't marry Scotty, I would spend the rest of my life alone.

Chapter Eighteen

PLAYING WITH FIRE

A can of worms opened, and Scotty's insecurities sprouted like dandelions when I said, "Michelle said the engagement ring would be beautiful if it were a full carat." That was the wrong thing to say. As soon as the words left my mouth, I regretted sharing them.

He became irate, put his hands in his pockets, and leaned against his vehicle. "Tell Michelle to buy the ring for you. I've been wondering if you two are lesbians."

My mouth gaped as he continued.

"You are very unappreciative! You don't appreciate all that I do for you. I told you this is the most I can afford to pay for a ring right now. Any other woman would be happy that I'm buying her an engagement ring. Why do you need a full carat? Are you trying to get one bigger than your girlfriends? You sound like a gold digger!"

A tear sneaked down my cheek, and I wiped it, stammering as I tried to interrupt his ranting, "I like the ring. I was only sharing what Michelle said –"

Once Scotty started venting, I couldn't get a word in edgewise. "You've got the wrong man, baby! I am not buying a wife! You can give the ring back if you don't think it's big enough!"

I glanced around to see if my neighbors were listening, and seeing none, I waited for him to calm down, and we went inside my house.

The diamond looked more prominent after wearing it for a while, and I got used to it. Looking back, I wish I had given it back to him and moved in another direction with my life. But I didn't, so I'll go on with how I married the man I felt was Satan's son.

Mesmerized by him, his confidence and enjoyment of life, and loneliness possessing me, I wrote in my journal that I wanted to be cuddled and was considering staying over at Scotty's place the next time that he asked me.

The devil read my journal, heard my loneliness mutter, and went to work to make it happen.

I worked the night shift at the hospital every other Friday and Saturday night. Scotty encouraged me to sleep at his place on the nights I worked the third shift, rationalizing that the hospital was closer to where he lived, and I could get an extra two hours of sleep by staying there rather than driving to my home and back to the hospital.

He said, "I can also make sure you're safe going to work."

It made logical sense, and I wanted the extra hours of sleep. I relinquished and started sleeping at Scotty's house every other Friday and Saturday evening before I went to my night shift job. He prepared dinner before I went to sleep and a lunch bag ready when I left for work.

During all our past time together, Scotty had not sexually touched me. He only kissed me on the forehead or cheek or pecked my lips. The closest Scotty had come to suggesting intimacy was caressing my hands and rubbing my shoulders once or twice. He had done nothing to indicate that he wanted sex.

But, every action starts with a thought, and Satan planted the image that I was lonely and wanted to cuddle, even with a man twenty-five years older than me.

Beelzebub had heard my words about feeling lonely and desiring a companion to hug, kiss, and cuddle, and I was thinking about cuddling with Scotty. Satan knew the lustful, sexual spirits inside me when I wasn't aware of them. He set me up in an attempt to destroy me.

By February 1999, I was eating dinner Monday through Sunday with Scotty, and we went through the same scenario Monday through Thursday before I left for my home. He would say, "It's too late for a lady to be out alone, and I'm afraid for your safety."

I would reply, "Scotty, I have lived in that neighborhood for fifteen years. I'm cautious when I pull into the garage and enter my home. I'll be okay, don't worry."

We would negotiate back and forth for thirty minutes, and he would say, "This feminist movement has made you women think you can handle anything. Go ahead but be very careful. Don't go home if someone is following you; don't pull into your garage if anyone is loitering around your or your neighbor's house. Don't forget to call me to let me know you made it inside safely."

I would kiss him goodbye and call him when I was secure in my home.

That night, we went through our usual scenario as I prepared to leave. But as I walked out the door, Scotty put on his jacket and said he was trailing me home to ensure I got into my house safely. "I heard about a rapist attacking single women in their homes on the news, and I don't want anything to happen to you."

To no avail, I tried to convince him that he didn't need to trail me home. "Scotty, I have lived alone for fifteen years. I don't want anything to happen to me, either. I'll be cautious, I promise."

He wouldn't listen to my reasoning and followed me to my vehicle, opened the door so I could slide in, and wobbled on his cane to his Lincoln Continental, yelling, "I'm going home with you and making sure you get in the house safely."

"Scotty!" I stepped from the car and headed to his front door. "Let's go back inside." Once inside, I said, "Take off your jacket, and let's talk."

He removed his jacket and threw it on the sofa.

"I'll call you as soon as I get in the house."

He folded his arms across his chest and tilted his head.

"I don't want you to leave the warmth of your home to trail me home and then have to come back to your own house."

He stood like a statue with his arms crossed and head tilted.

I sighed. "Well, I guess I'll stay over if this is the only way to keep you from leaving." My lips twisted from side to side.

The one night unfolded into every night. He slept on the sofa initially but magically ended up in bed one night. There was no sex, and he seemed content with having me beside him.

But I was getting caught increasingly in the trap; spending every night with him was playing with fire when I had made a celibacy vow.

How could I expect to remain celibate, spending so much time alone with a man every night, even if we were not having sex? I was dancing around an inferno, and I would get scorched.

Satan would whisper, "But you are not having sex."

And I tried to convince myself I was safe because I was not breaking my vow.

Spending every night with Scotty and sleeping in the same bed with him was dangerous, but I enjoyed the companionship and a body beside mine.

Since February, we had been sleeping in the same bed without having sex, so I felt safe. I honestly believed he was not interested in sex and just wanted a companion. I again ignored the warnings from the Holy Spirit to stay at home. I dangled too close to the edge of sin. And I didn't heed the Holy Spirit's voice.

On a rare, humid spring night in March, his air conditioner broke, and the ceiling fan seemed to blow hot air. Scotty stripped down to his boxer shorts and urged me to strip down to my underwear to cool off, wiping sweat off his face and chest with a towel. "Are you afraid that I will rape you or something? I know you're sweltering in those clothes. I haven't touched you inappropriately since we've been together, so what makes you think I will do something to you tonight?"

I didn't answer but continued to wipe the sweat off my face while fanning myself with a magazine, thinking about going to my air-conditioned home and inviting him to my house. However, it was after 1:00 a.m.

He stared, wiping sweat from his face but making no more comments.

After tossing and turning for about thirty minutes, I finally fell asleep.

I thought I had an erotic dream but awoke to him caressing my inner thighs and saying how beautiful I was. When I pushed his hands away, he tickled me. We wrestled, and I ended up straddling his body. Before I realized what was happening, we were making love. The following day, feeling I had disappointed Yahweh, I went home vowing never to spend another night at Scotty's, understanding that Satan can get to us if we are vulnerable and open our minds to his lies and deceptions.

I was still a saved, believing, Holy Spirit-filled, churchgoing Christian lady. I do not believe the Holy Spirit left me. I think I ignored the Holy Spirit dwelling within me—the warnings, the signs, the nudging, the "something is not right" feeling. I knew God still loved me and would forgive me if I repented of my fornication and stopped doing it. I was angry with myself for letting it go that far. I was furious with myself for not heeding the warnings of the Holy Spirit.

I was enraged with Scotty. If he genuinely and sincerely cared about me as a Christian lady, he should not have let it go that far since I had told him about my celibacy commitment.

He could have said, "Let's wait until we're married to have sex and not get ourselves sexually stimulated; let's not spend so much time together alone. Why don't you stay at your house, and I'll stay at my house at night, so we won't be tempted to have sex."

I had proudly written in my journal several times that we had slept in the same bed every night and didn't have sex. After over a year of dating, he had not touched my breasts or private area, and I thought he wasn't interested in sex and only wanted a companion.

Scotty said he didn't attempt to have sex because he respected me and wanted us to keep our vows to remain celibate until we were married. *What happened to us keeping our vows to stay chaste until married?* He and his dad, Lucifer, set me up, and I fell for it, hook, line, and sinker.

I tried to blame God. "How did this happen, Father? Why didn't you stop it, Holy Spirit?"

And then I tried to justify it, "I'm in love. Or is it love or lust of the flesh? Do I love Scotty or enjoy the touch of a man so much that I think it's love?"

Satan's trickery and my guilt from fornication deceived me into thinking it was love. As I glanced over the year, I shuddered when I saw how I was such a sucker for Satan's manipulations.

I remembered a conversation with a work friend that should have opened my eyes. Bea had said point blank. "My boyfriend, Bobby, behavior is similar to Scotty's – jealous, insecure, and controlling – I'll never marry Bobby. Scotty and Bobby are not the types of men you marry."

My eyes widened, and I stopped in my tracks. "What do you mean?"

"They are good boyfriend material and will do anything for you, paint your house, fix your car, and scrape snow off your car, but both are too jealous and controlling."

"I think Scotty will change after we're married. He loves me so much; he's just afraid he might lose me."

Bea's head shook. "That's what I'm talking about; he should be secure enough to know he won't lose you." She tapped my back. "You go for it, but I am not marrying Bobby."

We strolled silently for several moments, and then I said, "We've been dating for over a year, and I've not looked at another man. I might as well marry him since he wants to marry me, and we're always together anyway."

"You do you. And I hope it works out," said Bea, her head shaking.

Chapter Nineteen

FOOLISH LESSONS

Our relationship continued as it had been for the past sixteen months, and I didn't share my concerns with Scotty. Whenever I looked at Scotty's negativity, a voice said that I should look for Jesus and goodness in others, "No one is perfect."

I then rationalized that we all have faults, *no one is perfect,* and as a Christian, I should search for the good in people rather than the bad. The devil twisted my mind to view only one side of a coin: heads and ignore tails, creating a one-sided view of Scotty's behaviors. People are three-dimensional and have good and evil, negative and positive, and everyone has faults.

The cold of winter had wafted away, and yellow sunflowers filled my backyard as the spring season dashed in. The dreariness of the cold Midwest winter and spring fever warming my body made me want to get away to a hotter climate for a few days. At Saturday morning breakfast, I said, "Shirley and I have been discussing flying to Vegas to get away after the cold and snowy winter we had." My face cast downward, and I toyed with the menu. "We plan to fly out on a Thursday and return on Sunday." I glanced up, still fiddling with the menu.

Scotty raised an eyebrow and frowned. "What are you going to do in Vegas besides gamble?" His lips tightened as he spoke, "I thought you didn't go to casinos."

"I don't go to casinos. We want to get out of Madison for a weekend. I think I'm getting spring fever," I said, singsong. "Besides, you can do many things in Vegas besides gambling—relaxation, theater, shows, shopping. I heard that Vegas is family-friendly now. They even have a gospel crusade there annually."

Scotty took a bite of turkey sausage and mumbled, "Uh huh."

The following Saturday, at breakfast, he gave me an envelope. "Here's something to help you get rid of that spring fever."

My mouth gaped when I opened the envelope, and my eyes widened. Inside were two tickets to Vegas for the last weekend in March.

I rubbed my hands, beaming excitedly, "Are these really for me? Thank you so much, Scotty. I do need to get away. The three jobs have been stressing me out lately."

Scotty smiled tightly before responding, "You can take one of your sisters or Shirley. It's a gift to you, and you can take who you want, as long as it's not another man."

I stood up, leaned over the table, kissed him on his lips, and thanked him again. "I'll take Shirley since she and I already discussed going to Vegas."

Scotty said gruffly, "I said you could take whomever you want to. Apparently, you don't want to take me since you didn't ask me to go with you."

My breaths increased as I gave a high-pitched laugh, and I gazed down momentarily, gathering my thoughts. The correct response had to be accurate, or the situation would worsen. Flashing a broad grin, I said, "I would love for you to go with me, Scotty, but I don't think it would look good for us to go to Vegas together; you know that most people call Vegas 'Sin City.'

"Before you say anything, I know you don't care what people think, but I do. I'm trying to live a Christian life, and appearances can be deceiving. I don't want to be responsible for destroying one of the young adults' lives from my church, who may be observing my lifestyle. They won't know that you and I didn't sleep together and will think it's okay for them to go on a trip together and share the same room. Do you understand what I'm saying?"

He shook his head. "I don't understand what you're talking about, and what you're saying doesn't make sense. But if you don't want me to go with you, that's fine." As an afterthought, he said, "I'm a big boy. I can handle rejection."

Deciding it was best to change the subject, I talked about challenges at my jobs and how tired I was of working three jobs.

Scotty was sullen and quiet for the rest of breakfast but did not create an ugly scene.

The last weekend in March, Shirley and I watched children playing games on the Vegas strip with adults, on tours, at family-friendly shows, and at the pool. Even with all the city tours and performances, we got a little rest and slept late, which I had not done for a long time. We pampered ourselves with facials, pedicures, massages, and herbal wraps, squeezed in four performances, and shopped.

After safely returning to Madison, surprisingly, Scotty did not interrogate me on my return. He didn't ask what shows I saw, what restaurants we ate at, or any questions about my Vegas trip.

However, his verbal abuse, uncontrollable anger, and insane jealousy magnified like a fly under a microscope after the Vegas getaway.

Did I high tail it out of the relationship and get as far away from Scotty as possible, realizing a relationship with a jealous, belittling, and explosive-tempered man was not God's desire for me?

No!

Yahweh's and my goal were to marry a respectful, trusting man, displaying temperance and self-control, all clashing with Scotty's behaviors of condemnations, accusations, mistrust, and volatile temper.

But I decided to pass the test, learn the lesson I needed, and not run away from another relationship. During our many arguments, Scotty planted in my mind that I needed to learn to communicate, stop running from relationships, and try to work them out.

I was determined to make the relationship successful, no matter the circumstances. I was a Christian woman, a praying woman, and a woman of faith. God heard my prayers and could change Scotty into the loving husband I deserved.

I forgot that God doesn't do anything against our free will, and Jehovah would not change Scotty unless Scotty requested intervention.

Chapter Twenty

HE MISSED HIS HEALING

T hinking it would do us good to hear some good spiritual teaching and preaching, I suggested we go to a Christian Crusade the following Friday evening. The Midwest spring wind was chilling at 50 degrees, and the cold chilled me to my bones. We parked a couple of blocks from the church, and Scotty ambled, leaning on his cane because of his bad knees, back, and several hip replacements. That particular evening, he seemed to walk significantly slower.

Not wanting to upset or embarrass him, I slowed to a snail's pace so we could walk together. Whenever he and I were together, I purposely walked slower, although my pace was quick and fast. It started raining before we reached the church, and I was only wearing a pantsuit and no overcoat, the cold ached to my bones.

After the rain started, my body felt like it was turning into a Popsicle, and unconsciously, my stride increased, leaving him farther and farther behind. When I realized he was about ten feet behind me, I stopped and waited until he was two feet away and told him I was cold and would wait for him inside the church, continuing briskly ahead of him, shivering, with arms folded across my shoulders.

He shouted in a condemning, condescending, sarcastic tone as other attendees rushed past him, "Go ahead, leave me; I thought we were together. I'll find a seat when I get in, and I'll see you after church."

I waited for him at the entrance, and we sat together, but he puffed up, sighed during the entire ministry, and missed his blessings.

I tell you the truth; he got angry about minor things. The minister prayed for healing for people with chronic arthritis, back pain, and knee problems—all of Scotty's issues. We had discussed the healing ministries, and he had said he believed in healing.

The minister's prayer was Scotty's chance at recovery and our miracle, especially when the preacher called his various ailments by name. I believed in healing for Scotty more than Scotty did, and I didn't understand back then that my faith would not override Scotty's faith. He would never receive his healing if he continued with grievances, anger, and malice.

Scotty was angry and resentful because I was cold and walked ahead to get out of the rain. He missed his blessing and healing because of his hard heart. Perhaps Scotty was embarrassed because he couldn't keep up with me and the others. Scotty never dealt with his issues, fears, or insecurities, instead making everyone else feel insecure, guilty, and unworthy for him to feel more significant than everyone else.

Instead of listening to the Holy Spirit and getting as far away from him as the east from the west, I began praying more intensely for Scotty and my impending marriage.

Chapter Twenty-One

CONFRONTED WITH THE TRUTH

Scotty's not grilling me like a prisoner of war when I returned from Vegas was the quiet before the storm. That Saturday, while watching a Steve Martin comedy, laughing until tears rolled down my cheeks, the buzzing phone interrupted my laughter.

"Hello," I said rapidly and with annoyance, trying not to miss any of the funny punch lines in the movie.

Shirley asked in a theatrical dialect, "Are you sitting down, Hannah?"

"No, I'm standing washing dishes and watching a funny movie. Do I need to sit?"

"Yes. Sit down. What I'm about to tell you may make you faint."

"Okay, I'm sitting. What's up?" My pulse rate rose, and my face warmed, praying Scotty hadn't done anything.

"I overheard Markus and Lenny on the phone talking. Scotty has been stalking Lenny at his job."

I inhaled deeply. *Not again.*

"I made Markus tell me what was going on. He said Scotty visited him several times at his office, and they had lunch together. Scotty discovered Lenny's office was in the same complex. He had been standing outside Lenny's office, in the parking structure near Lenny's car, and in the restaurant where Lenny usually eats lunch."

I tried to defend my man. "What's wrong with that? That's not stalking, just because they happen to be at the same places."

Shirley's voice snapped. "I know about Scotty trying to run Lenny off the road, Hannah. That's bona fide stalking. Lenny doesn't want Scotty anywhere around him, and Scotty doesn't have any business in the building unless he sees Markus.

"Anyway, Markus talked to Scotty about it. Scotty swears you and Lenny are having an affair. Markus thought the mature and reasonable thing was to get the two men together and let them talk and resolve the issue, thinking if Scotty looked Lenny in the eye and heard him say he was not having an affair with you, it would end this madness once and for all."

"Did they have the meeting?" I asked, my voice shaking.

"That's why I told you to sit down. Marcus, Scotty, and Lenny had the meeting. Lenny looked Scotty dead in the eyes and swore that he was not sleeping with you, that you were friends, and that's all, that he loves Adelai and has been with her for ten years."

She paused and sighed into the phone. "Scotty didn't hear a word Lenny or Markus said. Markus said it was like he went ballistic or something. Scotty threatened Lenny, told him he knew what was happening, and if you weren't giving it to him, you were giving it to someone else.

"Markus said Scotty's distorted face scared him when it darkened and twisted like something unnatural. Then Scotty started talking about women in a hostile and derogatory manner, saying you can't trust women.

"Scotty said the reason he had been married seven times, yes, you heard me right, seven wives, is that the women were not any good;

they were whores, drug addicts, lazy and wouldn't work, didn't respect him, and so much more that I told Markus I didn't want to hear any more. Did you know he had been married seven times?"

My head shook, and I answered so softly that I was unsure she heard me. "No." *He told me he had been married three times.*

"Markus said Scotty didn't take responsibility for any failed marriages or the situation with him and Lenny, and he blamed everyone else, including you, for everything wrong in his life. You better be careful, Hannah. That man has a lot of anger and resentment toward women. I'm not sure if he even likes women."

My body felt paralyzed. I couldn't move from the position or speak as I tried to reply. Shirley usually had funny stories to tell me about her job, husband, or son, so I didn't expect to hear anything about Scotty.

"Are you okay, Hannah? Do you need me to come over?"

I exhaled loudly into the receiver, finally able to move and speak. "I need to process all this." My voice stammered. "I, I'll be okay."

"Are you sure? Even for me, this is a lot to process, and I'm not engaged to marry him. I can come over and sit with you; that's what friends are for, you know."

"Thanks, but I need time alone."

"I'll call you tomorrow."

"Okay." I hung up the phone, speechless from what I had just heard. After sitting in the same chair for over an hour staring into space, I mumbled, "Scotty, Scotty, Scotty, what am I going to do about you? That's why you didn't have questions about my trip...." My voice lowered and trailed off. "You were focused on Lenny."

Part of me wanted to say the stories were lies, but my inner gut told me they were true. Scotty would never admit to doing any of them.

My heart and head battled, my core wishing to stick by Scotty and my head running logical algorithms. *How would it benefit Shirley,*

Lenny, or Adelai to make up lies about Scotty? You have known them ten years longer than you've known Scotty. You've witnessed Scotty's loss of control. There is no reason for your friends to make up stuff about your boyfriend.

Erratic and erroneous thoughts kicked the crystal-clear ones out. *They want to break you and Scotty up because he is intelligent, stands up for his woman, speaks his mind, and doesn't let anyone control him. Yes, that's it; the three are plotting to break up our relationship. They don't want to see me happy.*

The question that should have won the fight in my head is, *are you happy with Scotty? P*erhaps I deceived myself into believing I loved him and continued the relationship because of guilt over my sexual mistake and the desire to put my flesh under submission. Maybe I thought marrying him would make it right and assuage my guilt. Possibly, I wanted to punish myself for the error I committed.

Before retiring to bed, I shoved the conversation out of my head and decided to stand by my man. That was fine if my friends didn't want to associate with Scotty. I was going to marry him, and that was that!

Chapter Twenty-Two

REALITY STEPS IN

My spiritual being tumbled tighter into Satan's grip as he played with my mind, telling me that I was not a Christian, that God didn't love me, and that I was a heathen and a fornicator.

I was in such a fog that I couldn't see the forest for the trees; my thoughts were fuzzy, and condemnation and guilt stalked me. Still hoping my friends and Scotty would get along, I talked to Scotty about hosting a get-together. If I focused on other issues, I could escape the persecution of guilt and condemnation.

Scotty didn't have friends, which should have signaled that something was off kilter. But like anything else concerning him, I ignored the apparent neon illuminating signs that something was off with Scotty. When I discussed my friends, he'd say, "Friends can't be trusted. Why do they need to say they're your friend? People get close to you and then try to take advantage of you, screw your woman, and lie to you. I don't want to deal with that mess, so I don't socialize with many people."

After listening to his rant when I brought up the get-together, I said, "Forget it. It was just a thought."

His head tilted toward me, and he studied me for several seconds. "I'll do the bar-be-cuing if you want me to."

"That's okay. I'm not going to do it. It was just a fleeting thought."

Later in our relationship, I discovered he had ostracized everyone because of his temper, mistrust, judgmental nature, controlling behavior, know-it-all attitude, inability to take responsibility, and domination of all conversations.

I can't explain how Satan manipulated me into thinking Scotty was my soul mate, met all of my requirements to God for my partner, and that I was in love with him. Specific requirements for my husband were in my journal, and Scotty did not match one. A gap was left somewhere for Lucifer to slip a word in here and there and to twist things around in my mind until he eventually convinced me to believe his lies.

Even though my requests stated that my husband would love, cherish, honor, respect, and be proud of me, the devil's aberrations closed my eyes to the truth. I had also asked for a godly, saved man, no more than ten years older, physically fit, and we would be compatible physically, emotionally, intellectually, spiritually, and sexually. My request stated that my spouse would be my loving partner for life, my soul mate, and the man Jehovah created me to marry. The man who I would bring joy, happiness, contentment, love, peace, and prosperity to, the man for whom I would be his "good thing," like in Proverbs18:22, where the Bible states,

"He who finds a wife finds a good thing, and obtains favor from the Lord" NAS.

Scotty didn't meet my requirements; his characteristics contradicted my requests. After his claws snagged into my personal life, he relentlessly looked for more and more negatives to accuse me of and bring up during a disagreement.

There was much madness and craziness in our relationship that I endured. One Saturday evening, Scotty picked me up from my small business. Being early, he came into the building, sat directly behind my desk, and waited for me to close up.

A young male employee, my son's friend, waved and said, "See you later, Ms. Cotton," as he walked through the sliding doors.

As soon as the gentleman stepped outside, Scotty asked, "Did he call you honey?"

For a moment, no words came, my brows creasing, contemplating whether I should respond or pretend I didn't hear the question. After a moment of silence, I decided it would be worse if I didn't reply, so I said, "Of course, the young man didn't call me honey. Why would he call me honey?" I heaved. "No, Scotty, he didn't call me honey. He said, 'See you later, Ms. Cotton.'"

He crossed his legs and said nothing. He had heard clearly what the guy said but liked playing mind games and observing my response.

Another time, we went to one of the ethnic festivals on a sunny Saturday afternoon with the temperature in the low 80s and the sun playing hide and seek behind the clouds. As we strolled, a male colleague I worked with at my part-time job waved as we approached. Without thinking, I gave him a shoulder hug and introduced Scotty. For several minutes, we chatted about community events, and he asked me to call him because he needed my expertise on a project. There was no flirtation or inappropriate behavior, and the conversation was strictly professional. Scotty stood beside me, leaning on his cane, listening to the discussion.

When my associate moved out of earshot, Scotty began yelling and swearing. "I know that guy was one of your old boyfriends. I watched the way he looked at you."

My head faced the ground as other festival attendees passed, gawking and moving away from the shouting scene.

Scotty shouted, "You disrespected me by talking to a man in front of me and saying you would call him."

My mouth flew open while I stared at the dirt, face flushing and hoping the shouting would stop if I didn't say anything.

After his anger flew away, we walked the festival grounds for another hour, with him buying African outfits and jewelry for me. Instead of dropping me at home, he drove to a video rental store different from where he had said the young man caressed my hand. He suggested we spend the evening watching movies as though he had not embarrassed me at the festival.

A man in his twenties, who had interned at the school, was in the video store. He said hi, and we discussed his future, wife, and family. When Scotty and I were exiting, the former intern was coming back into the store and smiled broadly as he held the door open for me.

Scotty ogled him up and down, non-smiling, non-blinking, with fire almost coming from his eyes. I closed my eyes and exhaled, knowing we would fight about the man. As he slid behind the steering wheel, Scotty started yelling and demanded to know who the man was. I could not remember his last name but gave his first name and explained again that he was a former intern at the school.

Scotty said, "You're keeping the fella's last name from me because you've got something going on with him." He cleared his throat. "And you say you're a Christian. You're a big liar. I thought you were different. I thought you were better than the rest of them. I thought you were a lady. You're a big hypocrite."

He knew I was practicing my Christian beliefs, and guilt would wrap me up if I did anything contrary to God's desire. Scotty knew which buttons to punch and what would cause me pain, like calling me a liar or a hypocrite, because I always tried to be honest in my dealings with people.

This argument was no different than the others. As usual, Scotty attacked my character and morals. I couldn't get one word in edgewise because he talked non-stop and didn't listen. After several interruptions from him, when finally able to speak, I said, "We can sing at the same time, but we can't talk at the same time." I waited for him to stop yelling and then tried to have my say.

He repeated, "You disrespected me again and don't respect yourself either. You act like a whore, just like other women." His head shook. "I thought you were a lady." He glanced at me. "I'm no fool and will not be made a fool of."

As he drove back to his place, he argued about my liaison with the intern, and by the time we reached his apartment, Scotty didn't remember much of what he had said. After he calmed down, he denied saying mean and cruel things when I confronted him about his behavior.

Shaking angrily, when we got to his house, I jumped out of his Lincoln, hopped in my Lexus, and drove home. You would think that would have been enough abuse for me to say, "Enough is enough." Right? Not me; I was tough as steel and could handle words. "Sticks and stones may break my bones, but words don't bother me."

Chapter Twenty-Three

SELF-DECEPTIONS

I told myself that Scotty's comments were only words, and he didn't mean them. Sometimes, I wondered if Scotty had a split personality because he vehemently denied saying and doing most of the nasty things once he calmed down, as though he genuinely didn't remember. I'd make excuses for him, "He was just upset because he thought I deceived him and was being dishonest with him. Once he realizes he can trust me, everything will be okay."

I constantly justified Scotty's behavior instead of accepting what I saw and heard. I knew better in my heart and spirit, but Satan's whispers filtered in and covered common sense. I was buying what Lucifer wanted me to believe.

After the video incident, I didn't talk to Scotty for a couple of days because the pain from his last explosion hurt to my core. The kettle was brewing inside me, and the feelings of smallness, insignificance, and devaluation intensified. When I wouldn't speak with him, he sent chrysanthemums the first day and purple and white orchids the next.

On the third day, Scotty called from a different phone, and his name didn't show on my caller ID. When I answered, he broke down crying and admitted that he struggled with mental health issues. Scotty didn't apologize but said he acted the way he did because he loved me so much and feared losing me. He asked for my forgiveness.

My heart went out to him because I had never seen Scotty defense-less. I decided to forgive him and meet him for dinner, and he gave me a diamond and sapphire tennis bracelet.

But that did not stop him from bringing up the incidents at every opportunity. Whenever we disagreed, he brought up the barbecue and hotel incident and included the festival and video incidents in his complaints against me.

Of course, we started talking again, and I resumed attending church with him and going to breakfast and dinner with him. Because of his hip and knee disability, he couldn't bowl, dance, rollerblade, bike, ride horseback, or even walk with me. Eating, concerts, and church was our favorite pastime together.

Scotty didn't pressure me for a wedding date, satisfied with me wearing the engagement ring to keep other men from approaching. Therefore, we had not set a date for the nuptials. My goal was to fit into a dress handed down by my grandmother, and if the extra weight surfaced, my grandma's dress was out of the question.

The thirty pounds I had lost by cutting out sweets and junk food crept back onto my body, eating breakfast and dinner almost daily with Scotty. The vision of wearing my grandmother's dress as my bridal gown was slowly slipping away.

We attended multiple social and church functions. Scotty perpetually said or did something to embarrass me, like overtalking me when others listened to my ideas or following me to the ladies' room.

If he didn't say or do anything at the event, he argued, shouted, accused me of acting like a whore, and interrogated me about every person who talked to me. "Who was the fellow in the straw hat talking to you? Where do you know him from? What were you and the couple talking about in the back? Why were you in the bathroom so long? What were you doing in there? Did you meet some no-good hick in there?"

He'd end with, "You embarrass me every time we go out together," after describing detail by detail how I embarrassed him or myself, disrespected him or myself, or flirted in front of him. He accused me of having an affair with someone at every event we attended; I don't know how he thought I had time to work with so many affairs brewing.

Afterward, I regretted attending the function with him, but I continued to go. I had made my decision to make this relationship work. No matter what happened, I swore to work through the problems and not end the relationship.

I would not end the courtship with Scotty if I felt we were unequally yoked as I had done in previous relationships because the man's views and personality differed from mine.

Subliminal thoughts told me I was acting too holy and sanctimonious and would never keep a man if I broke up with him due to personality differences.

I continued in the relationship through all the madness while working three jobs. Scotty phoned daily to say good night, even if he had called me nasty names before dropping me off. When he arrived home, he always telephoned and said in a honeyed, deep voice, "Good night, and I love you."

Perhaps the daily calls to say he loved me reeled me in like a catfish.

Chapter Twenty-Four

PLAYER'S GAMES

S cotty knew all of the *players'* games. I know because he told me one day in anger that he was the Master of Game playing and I would never win. After declaring that I was not being honest with him, he gave a crooked smile, looked into my brown eyes, and whispered, "Let the games begin."

Scotty and his dad, Lucifer, had me deceived, and I was hooked into his deceptions, thinking that I loved him, that he was the answer to my prayer, and that I must marry him. The amusement had begun for Scotty. He was drilling and dueling with my mind and trying to control me however he could.

One game he played was accusing me of buying clothes ahead of time, keeping them in the back of the closet or the trunk of my car as one of his conditioning tools. "I'm hip to every game out there, sweetheart. You tell me you're shopping, but in reality, you're meeting your lover, using the new clothes in the back of your closet or trunk of your car as evidence that you went shopping."

If I wore an outfit he hadn't bought, he quizzed me about it, "When did you get that? I haven't seen that before. Where did you get that?"

You get the idea. It didn't make sense because Scotty didn't know every item in my wardrobe closet. Honestly, I would never have thought of buying clothes ahead of time and using shopping as an excuse to see another man. I am not one of those women who like to shop. When I buy something, I wear it the following week.

Another brainwashing technique he used was manipulating me into telling him about my whereabouts for every minute of the day. After the engagement, he started questioning my daily activities, and if I weren't home precisely the second I'd told him, he would yell and attack my character. He called my house exactly when I said I would be home.

If I said I would be home at 8:00 p.m., he phoned every five minutes until he reached me. By then, he had worked himself into an angry frenzy. Heaven forbid if I stopped by the grocery store or got stuck in traffic and was ten minutes later getting home. I tell you the truth; the more I tried to please Scotty and do what he wanted me to do, the more demanding he became.

Scotty's jealousy and mistrust multiplied because he knew all the devious and unethical things he had done and was expecting payback for his misdeeds. He knew all the games he had played and expected to start reaping what he had sowed. He had shared bits and pieces about his affairs with married women when he was single and his entanglements with some of his female bosses. I suspect he anticipated some man to play around with his woman as he had done with other men's partners.

Skilled in his sport, during a telephone conversation, he said, "I worry about you when you're out late at night. I can't rest or settle down until you're safely inside your home. I call and let you know everywhere I go, so if something should happen, you will know where I am. I don't understand why you are so inconsiderate and selfish that you won't call to let me know where you're going or when you get home. You must be doing something wrong if you don't want me to know where you're going or when you'll get home."

I pretended to be engrossed in a movie and didn't reply. But that didn't stop Scotty. He bickered for weeks about this issue until I finally gave in to his requests and started calling him to let him know where I was going, that I was safely in the house, where I had been, and if I would be late getting home. I now know this was his way of keeping tabs on me.

Unbeknownst to me, after I got involved with Scotty, I was doing things slower, moving slower, getting up from sitting positions more deliberately, and acting like I had a degenerative joint disease or chronic arthritis.

While visiting one Saturday evening, my dear, sweet mother brought it to my attention.

Mom asked, "What's wrong with your legs that you're moving so slowly?"

I answered, "Nothing is wrong with my legs. Am I moving slowly?" My nose and cheeks wrinkled as I straightened my body and moved faster.

That was Mom's way of telling me I was mimicking Scotty's physical behaviors and changing who I was to please him. She also mentioned my longer and larger clothing.

I forgot to tell Scotty I was visiting my mom. When I returned home around 10:00 p.m., several hang-ups were on my landline voicemail. I picked up the phone to call Scotty, and it rang before I could dial out.

He shouted angrily, "Where have you been? I've been calling you all night, and you weren't home."

I ignored his angry tone and replied, "I went by my mom's house."

His retort was, "You drove *by* your mom's house, so where were you? You said you went by your mom's house, not that you were over at your mom's house. Sure, you went by, but you didn't go inside. You told off on yourself."

My palm smacked against my forehead in shock and unbelief.

He went on a rampage, talking about how I went *by* and not *to* her house, remarking, "I called your mom's house, and she said you were not there."

"You must have dialed the wrong number because I've been at my mom's all evening." I continued, talking over Scotty's voice for once, "And if you called and I had left, my mom would have told you that I had just left. You're lying, Scotty, or you dialed the wrong number." I exhaled. "How did you get my mom's phone number?"

He ignored my question, focused on the lying remark, and shouted, "Don't ever call me a liar again!" He hung up without saying good night and that he loved me but called back in thirty minutes and said tenderly and sweetly, "Good night. I love you."

After he got a foothold, he began toying with my mind, attempting to make me as mistrustful as him. He lied to my friends, trying to make me mistrust them, stop talking to them, and stop socializing with them in hopes of isolating me. He made innuendos and dropped a statement here and there, implying my friends gossiped about me and were not real friends. One evening, he said, "They say you shouldn't trust your enemies, but I think it's your friends you need to be wary of. Your so-called friend, Shirley, told me at their shop that I'm the best man you've ever had, and she hopes you don't mess this relationship u p."

He aimed to trick me to stop communicating with my friends. His goal was to isolate me from friends and family. He could control my mind more effectively if I was not talking to family and friends and only listening to him. Divide and conquer; his primary goal was to separate me from my family and friends so he could control my mind, activities, and life.

Fortunately, I knew my friends well enough to know it was Scotty's chess game, and I check-mated him. I didn't question my friends, I didn't mistrust them, and I didn't stop socializing with them.

But that didn't stop Scotty from still playing mind games. He evidently got an adrenaline rush from dominating me because the games were consistent and unexpected.

One Saturday night, sitting at his kitchen table eating before heading to my third shift job, out of the blue, he asked, "Who is Red?"

A crease folded my brows, and I shrugged. "Who?"

"Red. You were talking in your sleep, and you said, 'Ooh, Red, that feels good.'"

My eyes glared at him briefly to see if he was serious, and he stared back, non-smiling and scowling. "I have no idea who Red is; I do not know anyone named Red. It was a dream, Scotty, if I called his name in my sleep."

My head shook as the thought of him trying to control my dreams flustered me. He was trying to make me feel guilty about a dream. I don't believe I talked in my sleep, and Scotty made it up to see my reaction. He was always trying to catch me in a lie.

This action was one of his ways of entrapping me, observing my reactions to see if I stammered, flushed, or fidgeted, his verdict of whether I was telling the truth.

Thinking he had won control; his verbal attacks came more often. The next day, while he cleaned using a solution with an unusual smell, I started coughing and tearing and said, "That cleaning solution smells awful."

He responded, "It doesn't smell any worse than your stinky breath."

Shocked and speechless, my mouth twisted, and my nose wrinkled. Whenever I began to think it couldn't get any worse, Scotty did or said something to prove me wrong. My prayer was for my husband to love, honor, cherish, respect, and be proud of me, not say negative, nasty, hurtful things about me. I wanted my man to lift, encourage, and support me.

Well, that was not Scotty!

When I was with him, I must have been temporarily insane, bewitched, and voodooed. The times when I found the boldness to tell him he was the insecure, jealous, and controlling one, he yelled, talked loudly, and raved like a madman. But we continued to see each other, church together on Sundays, and every evening together at his place. His domination and self-assurance caused him to challenge me to find someone better. He subliminally fed me the thoughts that I couldn't do any better than him, even challenged me often to end the relationship, boasting I would come crawling back to him.

I did break up with him multiple times during our courtship but somehow returned to him after a few weeks.

Ironically, I unconsciously believed him and reunited with him after his words of love and commitment. His claws were so deep in my mind and spirit that I thought he was the best I could do to find a mate. It's incredible how the mind works. You can hear something so often that you begin to believe it, even though you know it's not true. My heart and mind said I needed to cut the relationship, let him go on with his life, and let me go my way.

I did not want to make decisions based on my mind and heart, so I waited for the Holy Spirit and Word of God to speak or give a sign. But, like a baseball player sliding into home base, I slid over the many promptings and Spirit-filled words that spoke to my spirit.

My mind knew Scotty was too jealous and volatile, creating more stress than joy. He always thought the worst and attempted to tear apart everything I loved, trying to prove me to be a liar, cheat, or whatever he had conjured about me after he decided I was cheating with Lenny.

Chapter Twenty-Five

BREAK-UP TO MAKE-UP

I didn't know how much more abuse I could take and decided to turn the relationship over to God and let Him handle it. So, I turned Scotty and our connection over to Yahweh, then took it back and tried to run it myself—horrible decision.

Before I went to bed that night, Scotty and I argued about another male he said I flirted with.

Fear prompted me to end the relationship after waking up sweaty with a racing heart and rapid breaths from a dream of Scotty beating me to death.

I telephoned him immediately after calming myself down from the nightmare, feeling I needed to end the relationship while terror wrapped me and before something dangerous happened. "I have tried to make this relationship work, but you don't listen. You suggest we communicate, but you do all the talking and expect me to listen."

"What brought this on? Did you wake up on the wrong side of the bed?" Scotty replied.

"I've been praying about our relationship and see it's not working out for either of us."

Scotty snorted. "Fine, if that's what you want."

The loud smacking of his slamming the phone hurt my ear, and then he called back within two minutes, talking sweetly and tenderly like he did when we first started dating. "Hannah, all relationships have problems. We need to talk about the problems and work through them. That's what you've done in the past: end the relationship whenever a problem arose. How will you ever learn to work through problems with people you care about if you stop talking to them?"

"That sounds good, Scotty, but whenever I try to work through the problem, you don't listen. You yell, bring up our past issues, and won't listen to a word I say."

Scotty said softly, "That's not true." He tried convincing me I was doing something immature by ending the relationship.

"Like last night, you accused me of flirting with someone I didn't even look at." I massaged my temples to cut off an oncoming headache.

"I didn't argue with you last night."

"If you say so. That's what I'm talking about. You don't want to talk when I bring up our problems; weeks later, you'll bring up the issue when I've forgotten about it."

"Why don't I come over and we can talk?"

"I don't feel like talking anymore." I made up an excuse to get off the phone by saying I needed to call my business. Before I could place the landline phone back on the rack, Scotty murmured, "Call me back."

Thirty minutes later, he called back, then five to ten times a day for the next seven days, leaving sweet messages, telling me his love for me made him act crazy, how much he missed me, and that he needed me.

After seven days of his messages, I backpedaled and reconnected with him.

Several times during our courtship, after one of his tirades, I told him we needed to end the relationship. He became delightful and charming, sending gifts and flowers and reeling me back. He pretended to listen and would not be as smart mouthed during those times, phoning daily and asking timidly, "Are you sure you want to end the relationship? We need to communicate with each other; you don't communicate."

After seven days or so of his sweet messages, gifts, and flowers, he and I would start talking again, and I would soon be back spending every evening at his house and going to breakfast with him every Saturday morning.

No apology from Scotty. No, "I will try to do better." Nothing. Zilch. He said what he needed to speak to keep him in control and get him what he wanted. When we got back together, it was as though nothing had happened. I was a novice. He had twenty-five years of game-playing experience over me.

Because he felt he was never at fault, Scotty never apologized. He often said he wasn't always right but was never wrong, either. Initially, I thought Scotty was being facetious, but now I believe Scotty was dead serious about never being wrong. When he got angry or upset, it was always my fault.

But I stayed in the relationship.

I couldn't pull away for some unknown reason, although I felt Satan was setting me up. I had lost complete control of my senses and fallen over the edge.

Perhaps it was guilt, depression, loneliness, or just thankful that I had a man, but all logic and spiritual perspectives had swooped like a chicken from a hen pen. My senses only perceived what Satan wanted me to see, not what was real, but what Satan wanted me to believe, ignoring all spiritual signs.

Scotty felt justified in correcting me on my clothes, hair, speaking, eating, and attitude but got very upset, malicious, and verbally abusive if I corrected him. He switched everything back on me if I tried to perfect or criticize him.

He'd ask, "Who in the hell do you think you are to correct me? You don't know squat and should keep your mouth shut! You have no etiquette or manners, and sometimes I think you don't have much common sense." Scotty continued the tirade until he felt he had torn me down sufficiently, and an hour later, Scotty denied he had gone off on me and acted as if nothing had happened.

During our courtship, Scotty hung up on me several times when I forced my opinion or denied one of his accusations. And he wouldn't call me back to apologize. If he called back, it was to say things like, "I can see why no one wants to be around you; you're too argumentative. That's why you can't keep a man; you like to argue over petty issues and cry over nothing."

My hands went into the air. Scotty was argumentative, prideful, arrogant, insecure, and fearful, but he smoothly attached his negative characteristics to me.

The next day, he'd telephone and accuse me of being rude, not calling him back, hanging up on him, and not returning his phone call. A quarrel always ensued about my faults before he hung up. Hannah was wrong, but not Scotty.

He was winning the mind game. He and Lucifer knew I was praying to become a better person, assessing myself. Hence, his statements like "no one wants to be around you, and you are too argumentative" made me turn the magnifying glass at myself. The thing is, I should never have accepted feedback from Scotty. Sure, I had plenty of shortcomings to work on and still have many issues that need dealing with, but I didn't possess the imperfections Scotty projected.

Looking back, I must have been very, very lonely and desperate for a companion.

I allowed this man to disrespect me and then let him call and convince me that everything was my fault. It was like I was under a witch's spell or voodoo curse.

Chapter Twenty-Six

BELIEVING SATAN'S LIES

Feeling like a garden snake in the wraps of a python, I desperately sought God's direction regarding Scotty.

Sensing Scotty wasn't my mate, I earnestly prayed for God to have His way in my life: to lead, guide, direct, and move Scotty out of my life if he wasn't my destined spouse. I wanted to hear from Yahweh, and thinking He would listen to me better if I prayed louder, glancing toward heaven, I shouted, "Speak to me, Lord. Speak to me, Lord. Speak Lord. Speak Lord. I am listening."

I wanted to be led and directed by God's Word and wisdom, not my feelings.

If I *was* listening to Jehovah, then I wasn't obeying. As noted in my journal, I wasn't following the guidance of the Holy Spirit. In my spirit, I knew Scotty wasn't my mate, but I was waiting for God to intervene.

I now believe my job was to minister to Scotty, not marry him. I was responsible for obeying the Holy Spirit and ending the relationship, but I expected God to remove him from my life. So frightened I would make the wrong decision, like a cat in a tree, I clung to the branches of affection Scotty offered and didn't decide.

Since Jehovah didn't seem to be listening to my pleas, I began praying for God to change Scotty and show him his character defects.

What I missed in the whole situation was that Scotty had to want to change, be willing to look at his imperfections, and seek God for himself.

Scotty believed the things he deluded me into thinking; he was a great catch, a good man, the best man I had ever had, and I couldn't do any better.

Satan and Scotty were messing with my mind so much that I got confused as to the will of God in my life and began believing Satan's lies instead of God's truth.

By now, you may be thinking that if I was an honest Christian, I would have listened to the Holy Spirit, obeyed the Holy Spirit, and trotted like a racehorse at the first sign of Scotty's bizarre behaviors. Satan and Scotty's twisted lie deceived me into thinking God would solve our problems; all I needed to do was hang in there. And because we were both Christians, eventually, our relationship would morph into a perfect marriage.

So, I hung in there, knowing I didn't want to be in a relationship or a marriage with mistrust, discord, jealousy, and insecurity. I knew this. I felt this in my spirit. But I couldn't get off the merry-go-round.

I concluded that I needed to work through the craziness with Scotty to build a stronger marriage relationship. I told myself that all relationships go through phases as the couples get to know and understand each other. I believed I was building our relationship by allowing him to vent his feelings as I stood like an armored warrior, displaying understanding and submissiveness. Reflecting, it was the devil's witchcraft. And foolishness on my part.

He'd have times when he was charming, kind, and listened. I suppose those peaceful times kept me with him, expecting *that personality* Scotty to reappear, but he never did.

Initially, he was thoughtful and considerate, said he always thought about me when shopping, and brought gifts often. Most of his presents were clothing items, and I now realize he was dressing me the way he wanted by buying my clothes. I was wearing skirts to my calf, blouses buttoned up to the neck, and both one size larger than my actual size. As you can probably guess, he convinced me they hung better and looked more sophisticated.

Scotty twisted all of my positive traits into negative ones. From his perspective, my confidence was arrogance. He convinced me that speaking up for myself was argumentative because he wanted to keep me submissive and under his thumb. Scotty said my friendliness was disrespectful, and my independence was stubbornness. My animated behavior became an embarrassment. When I changed to please him, humility became low self-esteem, and submissiveness was passivity. The crazy thing is that I believed him and tried even harder to be the *lady* he wanted me to be.

Chapter Twenty-Seven

BLINDED FROM REALITY

Before meeting Scotty, my image of myself was of a self-assured, opinionated, friendly, independent, hard-working female. I didn't want the titles of stubborn, dominating, aggressive, argumentative, rebellious, disrespectful, arrogant, or prideful. Scotty knew the tricks and used them to his advantage, pulling out a new one from his bag when necessary.

In every incident he felt someone had hurt, angered, disrespected, embarrassed, or mocked him, he held onto like a toddler clutching a security blanket. He didn't release anything and now discussed negative issues about his first wives as if they had happened yesterday.

He brought up the old problems in our relationship at every opportunity, enabling him to set me straight and give me a piece of his mind. I didn't want a part of his mind; he needed it all. For peace's sake and to avoid thunderstorms, I sucked my tongue and remained quiet on many topics I had strong feelings and opinions about to prevent arguments. Was that behavior the right thing to do or not? I don't know.

When I tried to confront him calmly, in a relaxed, discreet manner, he invariably flipped whatever I said. "*You're* just holding onto resentment. *You* don't know how to communicate. *You* never want to talk when I want to communicate. *You* are so insecure. *You* just like to cry and complain. *You're* so argumentative and think everything should go your way. *You're* a liar and a hypocrite. I don't want to talk about it, and that's it!"

No, I wouldn't say I liked it, and I didn't want a marriage filled with insecurity, jealousy, criticism, and negativity. I wanted a loving marriage filled with trust, honor, respect, humility, peace, joy, love, and happiness.

Leopards never lose their spots, and a snake is always a snake. I should have remembered those quotes. Scotty had survived for sixty-five years with his behaviors, and his spots were permanent.

Satan's web of deception closed my eyes to reality, making me see what he wanted me to see in Scotty. After vowing to remain celibate after the one incident of fornication, I tightened the chastity belt and was delighted Scotty didn't pressure me for sex. However, I often wondered if he was getting it someplace else. When I drove past his apartment, I often spotted teenage girls loitering in front of his door, which he said he paid to do chores for him. I didn't want to think evil thoughts or dwell on negative thoughts of pedophilic relationships between Scotty and the young girls.

So, I kept busy with my jobs and volunteered to assist Michelle in decorating for our ladies' spring brunch.

By the time we finished the last balloons above the door, the doorbell had rung, and Shirley strutted in, telling us a story about Markus. Afterward, the other ladies arrived, and we ate, talked, and laughed all evening.

For the first time in months, my body relaxed. I didn't jump and startle like a grenade was about to explode.

It was 10:00 p.m. before we knew it. I felt like we had just arrived, not wanting to go to my empty house and not desiring to hear Scotty's voice of accusations either.

While winding down, packing food, and preparing to head to our various homes, Adelai told us about the annoying calls she and Lenny had been getting since the beginning of the year.

She put fish, chicken, and veggies in a plastic container, saying, "Lenny and I have been getting five to six phone calls in the early morning between 3:30 and 4:30 a.m. Sometimes, the caller asks for a bogus person, but most of the time, after Lenny or I say hello, the caller threatens us with vulgar language and hangs up." An eyebrow raised, and she glanced sideways at me. "I was beginning to wonder if Lenny was playing around on me. I thought he was messing around with his old girlfriend again, and she was calling to aggravate him and me at 4:00 in the morning. Lenny swore that he was not playing around. Both of us are upset with being awakened every morning, so we paid to have the calls traced."

Shirley interjected, "Don't you have caller ID?"

Adelai's head nodded. "Yeah, but the caller blocked the number. That's why I thought it was his old girlfriend or someone Lenny knew because they blocked out the number. They knew what they were doing, and I knew it wasn't an accidental wrong number dial-up."

Michelle's hands went to her hips, and she leaned against the counter. "So, did you find out anything with the trace?"

"We're still waiting to find out. The phone company says they haven't been able to trace it to anyone yet." Her nose wrinkled as a frown covered her face. "They say it takes months to do a trace."

The women muttered how awful it was for anyone to call and wake someone up in the middle of their sleep and that it was plain mean. We finished packing our to-go containers, and the women walked into the hallway to get their jackets and purses.

Adelai and I were left in the kitchen, storing the remaining leftover food in the refrigerator for Michelle. She whispered, "It was Scotty, Hannah."

My hand went over my mouth, and I stepped back, not wanting to believe what I had just heard. "What was Scotty?" I knew my tone was brash, but I couldn't control it.

She stepped into the corridor to ensure no others were reentering the kitchen. "I didn't want to tell the others. They could trace the call, and the caller was your Scotty."

A vast gap opened between my lips, and my eyes enlarged. I then gazed toward the hallway to ensure none of the ladies were coming back into the kitchen. "Scotty?" I asked with confusion. "Are you sure it was Scotty and not a number close to his, or maybe they traced the wrong number?"

Having buried the other incidents with Lenny, I did not desire to deal with Scotty harassing them at their home in the middle of the night. *That's why he hasn't accused me of being with Lenny; he's badgering him every morning.*

"I'm sorry I have to tell you this after the road rage and stalking incidents, but the tracing company sent us a full report with all the calls listed for the past year. All the calls were registered to the same number belonging to Scotty Brian." She moved closer. "Lenny confronted him, but Scotty denied calling our house, said Lenny was a fool, and threatened to kill him if he approached him again." Her lips twisted to the side. "Surprisingly, the early morning calls stopped after Lenny confronted Scotty."

A loud exhale escaped my mouth.

Compassion flowed from her eyes as she gazed at me. "It was definitely Scotty calling us, Hannah. My question is, why? Why would he want to call us every morning for several months and not say anything? Something is wrong with him, Hannah. You better be very, very careful in dealing with him. He is like a hand grenade waiting for someone to pull the pin."

I sought advice from her. "Should I ask Scotty about it, Adelai? Or at least let him know that I know about it?" Before she could respond, I answered my question. "He will deny it, and if I tell him that you have records to prove it, he will say I'm taking sides with you and Lenny and am not supportive and trusting my man." My hands gripped the island countertop as I inhaled and exhaled several times to slow my accelerated heartbeat.

While rubbing my back and speaking softly, she said, "You have to make that decision, Hannah. Think about it and do what your heart says."

Clenching my teeth, with a faraway look, I turned but did not face her and said, "Yes, I'll think about it, and I'll also pray about it and see if the Holy Spirit directs me on what to do."

"You do that. I'm sure it will all work out okay. Lenny and I will stay away from the fool, as far away as possible."

My head wanted to attack her for calling my man a fool, but my mouth wouldn't open.

Shirley yelled from the hallway, "What are you two doing in there? It wasn't that much food left to put away. I'm ready to go, and I parked in front of Hannah, and now I'm blocked in. Come move your car, Hannah, so I can get home to my husband and child."

"I'm coming! I'm coming!" I shouted back and jokingly said, "Markus will be there when you get home."

Chapter Twenty-Eight

GLUTTON FOR PUNISHMENT

S cotty often bragged about his many surgeries, as though it was a sign of bravery, and went to surgery without second thoughts, several knee operations, and four hip replacements.

I assume he didn't follow post-operative instructions and needed a second surgery, which is why he had so many operations.

When the doctor suggested ankle surgery, away Scotty went to have pins placed in his right ankle. The surgery went well, without complications, and after two days in the hospital, he went home. After picking him up from the hospital and driving back to his apartment, I assisted him inside and set up the sofa for him to sleep on for the next couple of days.

He looked at me with crazed eyes and stated, "I'm not sleeping on the sofa," and started walking up the stairs, putting total weight on his right ankle.

Unfolding the post-op instructions, I read them to him and reminded him that he was to elevate his right ankle for forty-eight hours, no weight bearing or going up and down stairs.

He continued pulling his frame up the stairs, and my hands flew into the air. I sat on the couch and started watching television.

Scotty didn't follow any of the surgeon's or nurse's post-operative instructions, refusing to elevate his ankle, putting the total weight of his body on the right foot, and hobbling up and down the stairs twice a day.

To my surprise, he took more of the "PRN/as necessary" pain medications, taking two every four hours when the prescription stated one tablet *as needed* every four to six hours. His medicine clearly said one pill every four to six hours for pain only as needed, but he took two pills every four hours and wouldn't listen when I explained he was taking too many tablets and taking them too closely together.

A week after the surgery, he wanted to go to Ohio to celebrate another brother's birthday, so I drove him. A glutton for punishment, I sensed the trip would be a disaster but volunteered anyway. But knowing the relatives wanted their older brother at the party, I agreed to drive him. The other reason was I hadn't met any of his relatives and tried to meet them since I would be part of the family.

The trip was worse than Nightmare on Elm Street. After not following the doctor's orders for a week, Scotty sat on the back seat and elevated his right leg. As soon as I entered the expressway, the complaints started. "Slow down! You're driving too fast!"

When I slowed the vehicle, he shouted, "You're driving too slow. It'll take two days to get there at this speed."

I picked up speed and changed lanes too abruptly, and his right leg slid off the seat. He cursed. I glanced in the rearview mirror as he lifted his leg back onto the cushion. "You need to take driving lessons. Where's the water? I need to take another pain pill because of the pain you just caused."

Scotty didn't like the music I played. When I turned the air on, he was cold. When I flipped the heat on, he was too hot. The griping continued until we reached Ohio, and I hummed along with the music. That road trip experience should have been a sign of what would come. But, as I've told you previously, I was like a pig in a pig pen wallowing around in the mud of Scotty's wrath. As usual, I made excuses for his behavior.

On the road trip, he decreased the time between his pain pills and started taking two tablets every two hours. His speech slurred, he urinated on himself, and he mumbled incoherent and incongruous remarks between his grumblings. He gave me directions between his nodding, not knowing the address but remembering how to get to the house.

When he realized I missed our exit to the next highway, his head jerked up, and he yelled, "Idiot, you should have turned right." His chin dropped to his chest and then jolted upright. He shouted, "Make a U-turn at the next intersection."

So I could get back on the correct street, I made a quick U-turn, and he slid off the back seat.

Curse words flew from his mouth as he yelled, "You're *trying* to hurt me!" He hoisted back onto the seat and hollered, "You can't drive. You know you should have slowed down before making the turn. Now my ankle is throbbing, and I need another pill."

Uncomfortably calm, under my breath, I mumbled, "There's no way you can be in pain with all of the pain medications you've taken. You are such an evil, mean, and selfish person."

My eyes locked onto the rearview mirror, and I stared at him, sleeping and drooling. "I took vacation days to drive you to Ohio, putting miles on my car and doing all the driving when I don't even like to drive."

I returned my focus to the highway but continued venting softly since the teapot inside had whistled. "You are yelling and cursing me because I made a quick turn, which you told me to make." Steam blew from my nostrils, but Scotty was so high he wouldn't have remembered anything I said.

Once we settled at his brother's home, I avoided Scotty and spent most of my time with his sisters-in-law. Scotty was so out of it from the pills that it didn't make any difference to him.

I made it through the weekend, staying out of Scotty's way and watching him make a fool of himself.

The trip back to Madison was insignificant compared to the drive to Ohio. I had decided that I wouldn't let him upset me on the ride back and wouldn't get into an argument with him. He only had four pills left; therefore, he took fewer because he saved them for real pain. On the way back, he was like a different person, talking more civilly and respectfully.

Of course, he still controlled the conversation and argued, but he didn't curse me out as he did on the drive to Ohio.

A month later, he had another hip replacement surgery. Like a con man's mark, I made the colossal mistake of inviting him to recover at my house, thinking this would be an excellent time to assess what it would be like to live with him twenty-four hours a day, seven days a week.

It was dreadful!

But apparently not terrible enough to make this strong, courageous, invincible Christian woman break off the engagement.

Scotty had become my redeeming project, and I felt confident I could change and help him become more committed to Christ and me with love, patience, and dedication.

I should have considered that if I could not live with him twenty-four hours a day for three months, how could I expect to live with him for the rest of my life?

Chapter Twenty-Nine

TOUGH AS STEEL

While he recovered, so much happened that I don't know where to begin. Being a good fiancée, I accompanied him to surgery, visited daily, and picked him up when discharged. I brought him to my house and settled him in the guest room across from my bedroom. He came home with a walker, an indwelling Foley catheter, and a raised toilet seat.

During the first couple weeks, I cooked and took meals to him, cleaned around his catheter, and emptied the catheter bag when it became full because I didn't want him to get an infection. I also didn't want him to repeat the surgery by reaching, bending, or twisting too much.

Perhaps that planted the idea that I was obligated to perform the services.

One of those first days, while I'm on my knees, cleaning his catheter, he says, "You're not cleaning around the catheter correctly."

The first thought popped into my head, "You do it yourself then." My heart overruled, and I just exhaled and said nothing.

His feet smelled like boiled eggs hiding in his room for months, so I soaked, washed, and dried his feet. It was my choice to care for him, and not that I expected anything from him, but I at least thought he would appreciate the effort and say, "Thank you," realizing that I went beyond the call of a girlfriend to assist him.

Instead, to show his gratitude, he searched for things I didn't do, complained, and got angry when I didn't jump and trot to get something for him immediately. After using his raised toilet seat one night, he said, "The toilet seat smells like urine; it needs to be cleaned with bleach or pine sol."

My eyes didn't lift from the novel I was reading, and he hobbled back to his room. After working as a nurse for fifteen years, I knew how to sanitize a raised toilet seat and clean around a catheter.

He even made negative comments about the meals. "This has no taste, or this is too salty, or this fish is fried too hard, or these vegetables should have been cooked longer." There was no pleasing Scotty Brian.

Not thinking about the consequences, I set up his toilet seat in my bedroom for the first two weeks. Taking water pills meant he was up five to six times during the night to urinate. When he arose at night, he was very noisy, lumbering through my bedroom, waking me five to six times.

After the second week, I was so exhausted when I went to work that I finally moved the seat to the guest bathroom, which was more spacious than the one in the main bedroom.

Instead of understanding, his cheeks puffed, and anger whirled when he saw the seat relocated. He yelled, "You are one selfish woman. You shouldn't have invited me to recover here if you didn't want me at your house. I'll tell you what; I'll be moving out of your house tomorrow and move in with my brother."

He ambled out of my room with his walker, came right back in, and stood in the doorway. "Don't think I couldn't have my own house if I wanted. I've had several homes."

He leaned forward on the walker. "I live in low-income housing because my friend showed me how to switch my social security number and beat the system. I don't pay but a hundred dollars a month." His head tilted in my direction. "That's how I can afford to buy you everything I do."

He yelled as he turned the walker around, "And me and my brother's durable medical equipment business. So, I don't need your charity!"

By the time I ingested all he had said, a loud bang startled me when he slammed the door to his room.

Well, tomorrow never came, and his move never materialized. His brother didn't want him at his house again after allowing him to recover after one of his past surgeries, knowing how ornery and controlling he could be.

What was the problem with me asking him to use the guest bathroom? It was closer, larger, and more handicapped accessible than the one in the primary bedroom. I couldn't understand. Why was I labeled selfish because I wanted a good night's sleep to function at my job? It didn't make sense, and my head spun from the confusion.

Scotty did not go to recover at his brother's house as he threatened but stayed at my house for six weeks. Six horrific weeks!

Never in a million years did I imagine he would search through my personal belongings and read my journal while I was at work.

Yes, he did!

Unbelievable!

That should have been enough for me to say, "I've had enough. I cannot marry this man. He violated my privacy in addition to disrespecting me."

Would you believe that he bragged about reading my journal, said he would do it again, and dared to confront me about what he read about him? Some arrogance.

He glared at me and said, "Yeah, I'll read it again if I see it lying around."

"That was out of order, Scotty!" I hollered. "I've put up with a lot from you, but that was disrespectful, and I'm hurt and feel violated because my personal feelings are written on that paper."

"I don't know why you feel violated. You should have hidden it if you didn't want anyone to read it."

Still trying to understand him, I sighed and said, "Journaling is my way of clearing my head and organizing my thoughts." I glanced at him, hoping to see some insight or empathy. "It is a cleansing for me spiritually and mentally." My head shook. "I won't be able to write in my journal again for fear you will read it."

His head tilted, and his eyebrow lifted. "I will read it again if I see it."

Chapter Thirty

THE PATIENCE OF JOB

I should have thrown him out of my house then, but I was like a puppet in his hands. I wanted out, but when I found the courage to end our courtship, somehow, within a few weeks, I was back on the puppet string.

I tell you the truth; Scotty did such irrational and demonic things while recovering that I should have run away from him like a track and field competitor as fast as I could. The bars and chains of negative confessions imprisoned my mind, and the puppeteer was in control.

While still recovering at my residence, he called my job and asked where two champagne glasses with the year 1998 printed on them came from. It was appalling enough for him to contact me at my place of employment for a non-emergency, but to phone about something as trivial as where champagne glasses came from was ridiculous.

"I don't know what glasses you are referring to," I whispered. "We can discuss this when I get home."

He persisted in badgering me about the glasses. "They have the name of a hotel on them, and they have the year 1998 on them; you and I were dating at that time, and you were screwing around on me."

"I have no idea what glasses you are talking about. When I get home, I'll look at them and tell you where they came from."

He started cursing and said he should never have trusted me. He yelled into the phone, "I knew you were too good to be true."

"I can't talk now; my boss is staring at me. We can discuss it when I get home." I hung up before he could say anything else.

He telephoned right back. "You hung up in my face. What type of Christian attitude is that? Don't ever hang up on me again."

"I didn't hang up on you. I told you my boss was –"

He interrupted and wouldn't listen to common sense. "Don't hang up on me again. I'm warning you."

"I warned you that I was hanging up and, therefore, didn't hang up in your face."

Can you guess what he did next? He hung up in the middle of my sentence.

As soon as I walked into the door of my house, Scotty met me at the door, his face flushed and veins throbbing in his neck. He had thought about nothing all day but the glasses and that I was having an affair.

"Show me the glasses," I said, and we walked into the kitchen together from the living room. Scotty opened the kitchen cabinet and pointed to one champagne glass.

I picked the glass up, inspected it, and said, "I thought you said it was two glasses."

"It was two glasses; you hid one of them."

"How can you say I hid one of them when we walked into the kitchen together?" My eyes rolled, and a miffed sigh sounded. "Scotty, you have been with me every second since I walked into the house; how can you say I hid one of the glasses?"

He retorted, "I know what I saw."

"The one glass I'm holding belongs to my son. He and his girlfriend went to one of those romantic getaways to celebrate New Year's Eve. She kept one of the glasses as a souvenir, and he kept one for himself."

Scotty persisted, "There were two glasses, and you went to the romantic getaway with another man."

There was only one glass in the cabinet, but in Scotty's delusion and jealousy, he may have seen two glasses. Satan can deceive us into seeing things that are not there.

If he felt I was having an affair with another man, you'd think he would have ended the relationship and called off the wedding. Scotty was a master in mind games and creating illusions.

He came up with the most outlandish conclusions. One evening, while still recuperating at my home, he and I were watching television, and out of nowhere, he asked, "Are you a lesbian?"

Flabbergasted, my eyes widened, and my mouth gaped. "What made you ask me that question?"

"You always talk about that woman friend of yours, but I have never met her. It seems like a secret relationship, so you two must be lovers."

My lips pressed together as my head shook. "All my time is spent with you. You haven't met all of my friends." *Where did that thought come from?* I felt Satan slipped the idea into his mind to create more strife and division.

Another weird incident happened when I went home to check on him for lunch. When I walked into the house, he glanced up with a far-away look and asked, "Were you in the house earlier?"

My brows furrowed, a puzzled look on my face. I wanted to say, "If I had been in the house, you would have seen me." I politely replied, "No. Why are you asking me that?"

"I could swear you were here earlier. I smelled your perfume. I thought you were hiding, so I looked in the closet, under the bed (I had the hotel type bed, so there was no way anyone could get under the bed), and even in the toilet."

After he said he looked in the toilet, I didn't even bother to respond, thinking, *He must be taking too many pain pills.* It didn't cross my mind that those demonic spirits living in him may have been causing him to imagine, visualize, and smell things that weren't there.

I should have known then that Satan sent him to frustrate, belittle, dehumanize, and destroy me. But I was like a hamster on a running wheel, going in circles and not making the necessary changes.

There were so many tricks in Scotty's magic bag. One evening, as we headed to our bedrooms after watching television, he asked my definition of love.

We discussed the 13th chapter of First Corinthians, and I added, 'I love you' means nothing if your actions don't match your words. To me, saying, 'I love you daily, treating me disrespectfully, and disregarding my feelings is not love. You say you love me, but you don't listen to me, devalue me, make me feel like doo-doo, and abuse me with your words." I put my hand on top of his. "Reading my journal didn't demonstrate love to me. I would rather you show me you love me than hear you say it every day and treat me worse than your cat."

I John 3:18 (KJV) came to mind, but I decided not to recite it.

"Let us not love in word, neither in tongue; but in deed and in truth."

Trying to be transparent and honest, I hoped he would do the same, but he interpreted my words as negative instead of positive, as he did with all of our conversations. Scotty's viewpoint was supreme, and no one else's point of view counted.

He glared for several moments and then shouted, "So you're saying you don't love me, and you don't want me to say that I love you?"

"That's not what I'm saying, Scotty. I'm saying that actions speak louder than words. Don't just say it; show it."

"You only have to tell me once. You don't need to worry about me ever telling you I love you again because I won't."

He kept his vow and never again said that he loved me while at my home but continued to buy me clothes, jewelry, and flowers.

And he didn't call off the engagement.

Chapter Thirty-One

MADNESS! MADNESS!

Scotty did so many bizarre things while he recovered at my home that I can't discuss them all, but I will share a few more of the incredible things he did, which initiated increased breathing and sweating, just remembering.

One evening, while I was showering, he knocked on the bathroom door and began discussing one of his many issues with me. Because the water was running, I only caught bits and pieces of his conversation. When I didn't respond, he started yelling and shouting through the door, "You shouldn't have invited me to stay here if you didn't want me here."

Having no idea what he was yelling about, I finished my shower, put on my pajamas, and strolled toward the bed without saying a word, wondering what was so important he couldn't wait until I got out of the shower. When I spotted him blocking the doorway to the hallway, he locked eyes with me and glared. "Why didn't you answer me?"

After plopping in the middle of my bed, I said, "I didn't hear what you were saying. Why would you want to talk to me while I'm showering?"

My brows creased, and a scowl turned my lips downward. It didn't make sense. "What was so important it couldn't wait until I got out of the shower?"

I couldn't understand it—just another reason for him to yell and argue.

"Why did you invite me here if you didn't want me to stay with you?" He mumbled under his breath, turned, and hobbled to his room across from mine.

On many Saturdays, my only day to sleep late, he woke me at 6:00 a.m. to have these deep, serious conversations, discussing another thing he was upset about or the problems in our relationship.

One morning, super tired and fed up with his interrupting my sleep, I said in a bold tone, "You call me selfish; you're the selfish one for waking me up so early on the only day I can sleep late."

He retorted, "See, that's what I mean; you're only concerned about yourself and refuse to talk about the problems in our relationship."

He plopped on the end of my bed. "You're not considerate of my feelings, and I don't think you love me as you say."

Scotty had won again. Guilt pinched, and second thoughts came. Was I acting selfish for not wanting to be awakened to discuss issues that could wait? Perhaps I wasn't being honest with him about my feelings. But he always wanted to discuss something that displeased or upset him at his convenience.

As he recovered, his activity level increased, and he was allowed to drive. Scotty loved grocery shopping and came home with all types of generic junk food—cakes, pies, candy, cookies, chips, and ice cream - arguing that there was no difference between brand names and generics.

Therefore, he bought generic crackers, loaves of bread, cakes, cookies, peanut butter, pasta, canned goods., etc., etc. Brand names were my preference; therefore, I purchased brand-name products when I bought groceries.

The ironic thing is that he always, without fail, ate the brand-name products and left the generic ones for me.

It was the same with low-fat cookies. Scotty bought high-fat, high-sugar, high-calorie cookies, but hot diggity dog if he didn't consistently eat the low-fat cookies I purchased before eating the other sweets.

Another befuddlement for me was why he didn't eat the generic products he had purchased since there was no difference. Scotty was this humungous puzzle with missing pieces I was trying to put together.

After multiple incidents of not having cookies when I desired one, I asked, "Why don't you eat the generic products and high-calorie cookies since they all taste the same to you?"

His reply was, "What difference does it make? You're just trying to start an argument."

I couldn't understand at the time, and it baffled me. Looking back, I believe Scotty did many of those things to irritate, upset, frustrate, and see how far he could push me.

I tell you the truth; he was a wolf in sheep's clothing trying to break and tear me down.

While he recovered at my home, I believe Scotty was stalking me. At the time, I thought the incidents insignificant, but looking back and giving the incidents considerable thought showed he was following me and watching my every move.

On Saturday mornings, I was taking an eight-week flower arranging class, mentioned it to him, but never told him the location, instructors, or the school's name. After one of my sessions, after class, there was a note on my car from Scotty. *Scotty was here.* It didn't say to call him; he needed to see me or would not be home when I arrived.

He only scribbled, "Scotty was here."

Thinking it odd for a note only to say, "Scotty was here," I asked him if there was a reason he left the message when I returned home.

He peered over his tri-focal glasses. "No," and returned to reading the newspaper.

Many times, after I pulled up in front of my house or into the garage, he drove up and parked seconds later. Still not considering that he would be spying on me, I thought it just a coincidence that he and I pulled up simultaneously so frequently. I even commented that he had the extrasensory perception to arrive home at the same time I did nearly every day.

At the time, I trusted him and didn't suspect he would follow me around town, snooping. Sometimes, he'd have a cake or soda from the grocers, giving me the impression he had come from the grocery store. However, he often told me he was coming from a doctor's appointment. Unsuspectingly, I said after one encounter, "You must have a doctor's appointment every week."

Scotty snarled, "I don't go to the doctor any more than anyone else."

He hobbled across the hall to his room and slammed the door. Soft chatter came from his room. Curious about why he was whispering, I tiptoed to his door and listened.

Scotty said, "Don't sweat it, man. I'll be back to straighten things out in a few weeks." Silence as Scotty listened. "We're not going to get in trouble, man. They gave us their Medicare numbers and said it's okay to bill for DME as long as they are in on the deal." A loud sigh from Scotty. "Tell you what; I'll stop by and look over the account numbers to make sure there's nobody on the list that we didn't give some free equipment."

He must be talking to his brother, Moses—a sound of shuffling as Scotty headed toward the door. I ran back to my room and jumped on the bed.

Scotty poked his head into the doorway of my room. "I'm running out for a minute."

"Okay."

I wished to discuss multiple things with him while he lived with me, but fearful of starting an argument, I didn't mention most.

Like an elephant, Scotty never forgot issues and became defensive and argumentative when I wanted to discuss problems.

Weeks after the surgeon lifted medical restrictions, Scotty didn't shower and took sponge baths instead for some reason. The nauseating stench of dirty feet made me gag when he hobbled through the house. Having given him a foot bath that he didn't appreciate, I did not offer it a second time. His feet stunk like moldy cheese.

After dropping hints that his feet needed soaking, which flew over his head, I inhaled a long breath and said, "Sweetheart, your feet are smelling up the house."

His retort, "You can wash them if you think they smell."

It had been three weeks since he'd washed his feet, so they smelled worse than rotten eggs. At his timing, he eventually soaked his feet.

For weeks, the loud television in his room disturbed my sleep, and I was puzzled about how to tell him I could hear every word the actors said in my bedroom with my door closed. When I had my television up louder than he thought, he shouted from his room, "Turn that darn TV down; you must be deaf. I don't want to hear what you're watching; I'm watching the game!"

If I did the same thing, I'd be nitpicking. Scotty was such a hypocrite and had such a double standard. What was justified for him was not the same for everyone else. If I lovingly said, "Please turn the TV down a little." I was selfish.

Chapter Thirty-Two

MADNESS! MADNESS! AND MORE MADNESS!

There was no end to Scotty's madness. One morning, after getting home from my third shift weekend job, I was exhausted and just wanted to jump in bed. I didn't perform my usual routine: going to my bedroom, throwing my purse on the rocker, taking my work clothes off, and using my bathroom to wash my face and brush my teeth.

I stopped in the first bathroom and started my ritual to prepare for sleep. As I completed my face washing, Scotty slammed the bathroom door open and stood in the doorway like the FBI, making a bust.

A dark, bear-shaped silhouette screened his face, and he looked like a demon.

A raucous shout came from his mouth, "Why are you washing up before going to bed? And why are you using the guest bathroom?"

Shock, fear, and anger caused my body to freeze and my eyes to glare at him until the demonic shadow faded, not responding for a few beats.

I tell you the truth; Satan attacks us when we're tired, weak, hungry, depressed, and not feeling our best.

I was drained. I had worked two jobs all week and a third one that weekend, and my body cried for rest. A dormant volcano erupted inside me. I was in no mood to discuss why I used *my* guest bathroom before checking in with him first.

High-pitched, tremulous words flew from my mouth. "It's my house, and I can use any bathroom I want to!"

"You're taking the whore's bath!" he shouted, blocking the doorway. "Did you go to work last night?"

"You have no idea what I am doing in here. I'm not even washing up!" I screamed.

Scotty yelled, "You are washing up. What time did you get off work? Did you even go to work?"

Words tumbled from my mouth a mile a minute, spit flying through the air. "How dare you imply that I didn't go to work? I work very hard at my three jobs. You are staying here rent-free, and I haven't asked you for a penny. I have nurtured you and put my life on hold for you, and all you do is complain and accuse me of doing something wrong. I am exhausted and need your support rather than all the accusations and suspicions."

My eyes rolled in his direction. "You can go to work with me tonight if you don't think I'm going to work."

It was like I was talking to myself or the wall. Scotty didn't respond to anything I said, only yelled what was in his head, "I'm not gonna take no mess from you."

He added, "As soon as I recover from this surgery, I'm moving out of your house, and you can do what you want. But as long as I stay here, you will not disrespect me!"

"You are recovered! The doctor released you two weeks ago."

My arms crossed my chest in defiance. "You have no idea what respect is. You demand it from others but don't give respect."

I concluded that Scotty didn't like himself and couldn't believe anyone else could genuinely like him.

Having stayed two weeks longer than necessary, he blew his cover when he lost control. During the sixth week at my home, one Saturday evening, his jealousy got the best of him.

My older brother, Lonnie, was visiting from Michigan and stayed at my shop to close up with me. After closing, we jumped in my vehicle and drove to my mom's house, talking and laughing, and I didn't notice Scotty's Lincoln behind me.

As soon as I paralleled parked, Scotty pulled up, rapidly angle-parking his car directly behind me, and started shouting before Lonnie and I could step out of my car. "Who the hell is that in the car with you?"

I was surprised to see Scotty parked next to me, wondering how he knew I was going to my Mom's after work since it was a spur-of-the-moment decision.

It still had not dawned on me that he was tailing me. Smiling, I asked, "How did you know I was coming to Mom's?"

He yelled, "Who is the man in the car with you?"

Lonnie jumped out quickly, walked over to Scotty's car, shook his hand, and said, "Hello, future brother-in-law."

I'm guessing he used the phrase brother-in-law to tell Scotty he was not a threat. Scotty's eyes bucked and then went downcast, looking like a sick puppy. Words wouldn't come, and he started stuttering, not making sense and looked away from us.

In all the time we had been together, I had never heard him stutter, and that's when it hit me like a hammer across my head. *He was spying on me and had to be following me. How else would he know where I was going?* My armpits sweated, and a ball formed in the pit of my stomach, sending tinges of fear through my body. *How long has he been tailing me?*

He was so confident he had caught me with another man that he didn't try to hide his spying. He was busted. This game was over.

He was stammering because Lonnie and I understood that the only way he knew where I was going was that he was following me. Lonnie invited him inside, but he shook his head, his countenance pale and sheepish looking, still not making eye contact.

Did that make me take a second look at our engagement?

Scotty was my opportunity to prove that I was a woman of faith and watching him become a mighty man of God after we were married would be my testimony. I rationalized that he was a "bit" jealous, but after we married, the trust would come, and he wouldn't feel the need to spy on me. Neither one of us discussed the incident after that. When I returned home, Scotty had prepared dinner, washed dishes, and cleaned the house.

Relief! Relief! Relief! He finally returned to his apartment. After a week's intermission, I returned to my old routine of spending most evenings at his place. I guess I was crazy and mindlessly in love.

He informed me he needed to have the surgery redone after six months because he was too active. There would be no invite to recover at my home after the second surgery. I couldn't take another six weeks of him living with me. The light bulb didn't flicker that a lifetime of living with him would be torturous, like sleeping with a venomous snake.

Chapter Thirty-Three

CONFRONTED WITH THE TRUTH

Summer love and the summer heat were in the air. Winter had drifted, and spring breezed by swiftly.

I saw Lenny and Adelai at social events, but they didn't come to the table if Scotty was there. Having not heard more stories of Scotty trying to run Lenny off the road, stalking him, or making harassing calls, I assumed Scotty had buried the jealousy toward Lenny.

Singing with praise music and having a quiet, solitary night, I decided to pamper myself in the Jacuzzi with candles, incense, and relaxing jazz. The phone rang just as I was about to step into the Jacuzzi.

"Hello?" I said quickly.

"Hannah, I need you to come to my place now." Scotty's voice was flat and low.

"Scotty?"

"Who else did you think it was? I need you over here as soon as you can get here."

"What's going on? Are you sick? Should I call 911?"

He replied gruffly, "If I needed emergency medical services, I would have called 911. Just come over here as soon as you can. Okay?"

"All right, I'll throw on a jogging suit and get over there as soon as possible. But what's going on?"

"I'll tell you when you get here. Just hurry over here."

I hung up the phone, threw on a black jogging suit, and drove as fast as possible to the housing project without being stopped by a police officer. When I arrived, I jumped out of my car, hit the remote to lock the doors, trotted to Scotty's porch, and rang the doorbell. The door was ajar, and Scotty yelled from his basement, "Lock the door and come down to the basement!"

A huge tremble filled my body, and an eerie feeling possessed me. My body froze atop the basement stairs, wondering if Scotty had finally flipped and gone completely mad.

Multiple thoughts went through my mind: *What if he plans to kill himself and me? What if he only intends to kill me? No one knows that I came over here tonight. He could bury me in his basement, and I could be missing for months before they relate my disappearance to him.*

I exhaled. "*Calm down, Hannah,*" I told myself. *You're letting your imagination get the best of you. He is not going to kill you or himself. There is some logical reason why he had you rush over, and he's in the basement. Maybe he fell and can't get up.*

As my mind projected scenarios, Scotty yelled from the basement, "What's the problem? You can't find your way to the basement?"

Lenny's voice echoed from the basement. "Hannah!"

My hands went to my chest as I froze at the top of the stairs. *What is Lenny doing here at Scotty's?*

"I'm on my way!" I shouted as I slowly walked down to the dimly lit, musty, humid basement. My eyes first spotted the .38 revolver Scotty had shown me how to use in his hand. Then my eyes darted to Lenny, handcuffed to a plumbing pipe, and Scotty's hand pointed toward Lenny's head. I wanted to run back up the stairs and out the door. But I knew I couldn't show fear, or Satan would win, and I had to help Lenny.

A loud gasp sounded from my mouth, and then I yelled at Scotty, "What are you doing, Scotty? Have you gone completely crazy? Why do you have Lenny handcuffed and a gun to his head? What is wrong with you?"

Lenny was kneeling with his right wrist handcuffed to a pipe, his eyes wide, and sweat bubbling on his forehead, gazing from me to Scotty.

"What are you doing here, Lenny?"

Before Lenny could answer, Scotty turned the gun to my heart, his eyes squinting and the same black demonic silhouette screening his face that I'd seen at home. "Tell me the truth, Hannah; are you and this dude sleeping together? All I want to know is the truth. I am nobody's fool and will not be made a fool of. I have been to prison once for murder and don't mind going again if I have to."

My breaths became shallow and rapid as I huddled into a corner. *I thought you were joking when you said you had been to prison. And murder?* My breath stuck in my throat.

He moved to Lenny and pointed the gun at Lenny's temple. "How long have you been screwing my woman? I told you I would kill you if you ever touched or kissed her again."

Lenny gazed back and forth from Scotty to me, his eyes lingering as he studied my body language, waiting for me to convince Scotty we were not sleeping together.

"Why did you come here, Lenny?" I prayed silently for the Holy Spirit to tell me what to do. Time seemed to stand still, and the room floated around my head.

Lenny snarled, "I didn't!" He glared at Scotty. "I was forced at gunpoint."

My eyes darted back to Scotty as I prayed. After what seemed like hours, but in reality, was sixty seconds, Scotty walked back toward me, leaning on his cane. "Hannah, I love you and would do nothing to hurt you, but I will kill this dude if you are screwing around with him. Just because I'm old doesn't mean I'm a fool. I know what you younger women think about us older men."

Too scared to move closer, but realizing I must do something, I locked eyes with Scotty and pleaded with him to release Lenny. "I love you, Scotty, and you know I have not looked at another man since we've been dating. What possessed you to do this?"

Scotty stepped closer, his eyes still holding mine. He then gazed at Lenny. Lenny's face was apple red as he tugged on the cuffs and glared at Scotty.

I whispered, "Lord, keep Lenny's mouth shut until I calm Scotty and he removes the handcuffs."

Scotty stared back at me, put the gun in his pocket, folded his arms around my neck, kissed me on the forehead, and started sobbing. "I don't know what I'd do without you, Hannah. I love you so much. I don't think that I could live without you in my life."

"Release Lenny and let him go," I pleaded. "He has no relationship with me except friendship. He has been dating Adelai for ten years."

Scotty's countenance changed, and the darkness covering his face vanished. He looked at Lenny with one side of his mouth lifted, and his eyebrows creased as if wondering what Lenny was doing handcuffed in his basement.

I gently took the keys from his pocket and walked over to Lenny, a finger covering my lips, motioning for him to be quiet. I didn't know how long Scotty would be in this tranquil disposition. When I unlocked the handcuffs, Lenny jumped to his feet and rushed Scotty, knocking him to the concrete floor. They wrestled as Lenny tried to take the gun from Scotty's pocket.

Scotty hit Lenny in the face with a right fist, stunning Lenny and knocking Lenny to the floor. Before Scotty could raise his right elbow and pull himself up, leaning on one of the plumbing pipes, Lenny punched Scotty in the stomach and quickly hit the right side of his face multiple times.

I yelled, "Stop it! Stop it!" but neither heard my shouts. Then I heard what sounded like a firecracker, *boom*! And I screamed as Lenny collapsed to the floor. I rushed to his side to see if he was dead. Lenny glanced toward his left shoulder, indicating a shot in the arm.

"We've got to take him to the emergency room, Scotty."

Scotty pulled himself to a standing position.

"I didn't miss your heart by accident. I wasn't trying to kill you yet. We'll take you to the emergency room. But I'm saying you broke into my house, and I shot an intruder. Hannah will attest to whatever I say."

"Whatever you say, Scotty, let's just take him to the hospital before he bleeds to death." I grabbed a towel and put pressure on the wound to stop the bleeding. But the towel was quickly soaking with blood, and Lenny's head was wobbling; he was losing consciousness. "Say you broke in, Lenny. You don't want to die here."

Lenny thought for a second, then nodded. "Whatever you say, man, just get me out of this madhouse."

On the drive to the hospital, Scotty and Lenny agreed that Scotty was showing Lenny his new gun, and it accidentally discharged. The police officers accepted the explanation and filed no charges.

Chapter Thirty-Four

BRAINWASHED BY SATAN

After the basement incident, Adelai was upset with me and didn't speak to me for weeks. Shirley took us to lunch and mediated until Adelai admitted it was not me but Scotty who was the villain.

As a truce, I paid for her to attend a "Women of Purity" conference with me. She and Lenny had been shacking up for five years, and neither discussed getting married. I was hoping this conference would stir something in her. Little did I suspect I would also have to do some soul-searching about getting married and the type of mate I expected to spend the rest of my life with.

The conference leader broke us up into small groups of ten so that each person would have the opportunity to share their expectations. Instructed to write down everything we desired in a mate and discuss it in our small group, I twirled my desires and Scotty's characteristics in my head.

Surprisingly, as we convened back into the large group of more than one hundred women, the moderator asked us to take two minutes to tell other women our expectations. Thinking my requirements were honorable and achievable, I volunteered to be the first to share what I desired in my husband.

Standing and smiling in front of the group, I read off my criteria for a mate. "God is sending me my Boaz, a husband that loves, cherishes, honors, respects, and is proud of me. He will be no more than ten years older and physically fit. He will be my loving partner for life; my soul mate; the man whom God created me to be a helpmate for; the man whom I will bring joy, happiness, contentment, love, peace, and prosperity; the man for whom I am his good thing."

I glanced up from my paper. "You know, like in Proverbs, where the Bible states,

"He who finds a wife finds a good thing, and obtains favor from the Lord" Proverbs 18:22 (NAS).

I chuckled, "I will accept him if he is also ten years younger than me."

Laughter erupted in the room, and some of the women said amen.

Scotty was the opposite of everything I requested from God in my husband. Yet I convinced myself that Jehovah answered my prayer for a mate and continued my plans to marry Scotty.

With Satan's help, I brainwashed myself that Scotty was sent from God to mature me spiritually and prepare me to be a submissive wife. Since I was not looking for a husband, he found me, and he was not the type or age of man I usually dated. He must have been from God.

I now know that was foolish and unbiblical thinking. At the time, though, I thought I was in God's will. I can tell you that I did all in my natural power to bring joy, happiness, contentment, love, peace, and prosperity to Scotty at the expense of my joy, happiness, contentment, love, peace, and prosperity.

But he and Satan wanted my soul and my spirit. Satan was using Scotty to try to destroy my heart and will. It was not enough for me to give him all of the above; Scotty wanted me to love him how he wanted to be loved. To act the way he thought I should, to dress the way he desired, to style my hair the way he thought it looked best, and even to walk differently.

He said, "You try to throw your hips when you walk; just walk normally."

I assured myself he meant well and wanted his lady to speak correctly, dress appropriately, and carry herself queenly.

At the time, I didn't realize he was trying to make me into his perfect lady, and even with my total submissiveness, he wasn't satisfied. The thoughts came that he was Satan's son and would never be happy until he broke my spirit and soul and destroyed me.

But I felt powerless to pull away. I had unwittingly relinquished the power of the Spirit living within me.

We continued with our plans to be married, although the relationship was still very volatile, and he was becoming more demanding and controlling. I cannot explain why I continued with the plans to marry him after observing all the sad things about him I didn't like and experiencing all the verbal abuse. I was under a spell, believing verbal attacks were less significant than physical smacks.

I knew I didn't want to be married to an abuser and someone who didn't respect or honor me, yet I continued with the plans to marry him. I kept telling myself the lie that he would change after we were married, and I had invested too many years into this relationship.

For some reason, I foolishly believed his jealousy and insecurity were because we lived in separate homes, not remembering the insane jealousy he displayed while recuperating at my house. I thought once we married, lived together, and Scotty had me as his wife, he would be more secure in our relationship and trust me more.

Maybe I cradled those thoughts because I know people can change their behaviors if they want to, and I wanted to believe he would change.

Scotty shared some of the naughty things he did as a young adult. When younger, he loved gambling, hustling, drinking, carousing, cunning, and chasing women. There were multiple attempts to kill him and several run-ins with law enforcement. He said he was now a Christian, a new creation in Christ, a changed man, and didn't do those things anymore.

During one of our chats about his ex-wives, he'd said, "They were the wrong women. I've finally found my God-given mate in you."

I wanted to believe him and ignored all of the glaring outward signs. I later learned he was like a dry drunk; he had stopped the behaviors, but his thinking had not changed.

Don't get me wrong; I saw many of his negative traits. But there would be occasions when he was charming, treated me like his queen, and surprised me with gifts, flowers, weekend getaways, and concert or theater tickets. Yes, he could be very caring, loving, and concerned one night and ostensibly wicked and outrageous the next.

One night, while watching a newscaster report the rape and beating of a divorced woman, Scotty said, "If something were happening to you, I would be there in a heartbeat, running red lights and everything to make sure you're okay."

My heart melted within me. Here are some things that made me stay with Scotty: his apparent caring and saying the right words to make me feel special. However, I still questioned why he wanted to marry me when he had such negative feelings about my behavior and attitude.

I asked myself again and again, *why would he want to marry me when he thinks I am a liar? That I'm having an affair with another man? That I'm a phony? That I'm a hypocrite?*

I knew the verbal abuse, the yelling, the accusations, and the mistrust were not how a man should treat the lady he loved and planned to marry, and I knew this was not what I wanted. But I was lost in this maze and unable to find my way out.

I dwelled on the good times and continued to make excuses for his behavior. *At least he's not a wimp and doesn't let me or others push him around. He's not a woman beater. I do not doubt that he loves me. He's direct and to the point and doesn't bite his tongue but says what he thinks. Yeah, he's overprotective, but his jealousy shows that he cares. If he didn't care, he wouldn't be jealous.*

These were the sayings he used to brainwash me. He had said them so many times that I was telling them to myself and beginning to believe the lies—poor me.

Chapter Thirty-Five

DENIAL! DENIAL! DENIAL!

The more I submitted, the more abuse Scotty displayed. It was like he felt he had captured the prey and was now in total control, as though I was his property, lock, stock, and barrel. Scotty felt one hundred percent confident that I would never leave him and never divorce him once we married because I was a Christian. So he was secure in treating me like a possession and being verbally abusive.

When I tried to talk to him, he wouldn't listen and overtalked me. It was like talking to a table, chair, or lamp. There was such a double standard; he could say whatever he felt to me and was being honest, but if I said what I thought or felt, I was being negative.

By this time, Scotty and I were pretty miserable —tempers flaring, quarreling, not communicating or trusting—and that's not good in any relationship.

Unfortunately, we continued toward the altar—a massive mistake for both of us. I think I was just tired of being alone. Having been single for fifteen years, I was willing to settle for anyone to keep from being alone another year. Sorry to admit it, but I think that was the truth as I look back.

Unable to jump off the merry-go-round relationship with him, I began to view it as a test from Yahweh, thanking God for putting Scotty in my life and causing me to grow spiritually.

Being with Scotty made me pray more fervently and seek God more diligently to deal with his bipolar behaviors. Even though I understood that Satan was a defeated foe, and the greater one lived within me. While still going through the madness, I affirmed,

"You are from God, little children, and have overcome them; because greater is He who is in you than he who is in the world" I John 4:4 (NAS).

I wanted to believe that Scotty was now a Christian and would change some of his suspicious behaviors as he matured spiritually. I didn't see those changes, but I didn't want to be too hard on him.

Scotty still felt he had to get the other guy before he got him, letting anger, paranoia, quick temper, and mistrust direct his actions. He once told me he wanted to stab a motorist who gave him the finger and was hoping the man would stop at the red light so he could jump hi m.

Yes, he had stopped drinking, gambling, and partying and proudly acknowledged he didn't play cards anymore. He wouldn't even play Uno or Pitty Pat with the children.

But he still had the "Stinkin Thinkin" and dry drunk syndrome that drug addicts and alcoholics show when they continue to think and act the same, although free from addictive substances.

Scotty focused too much on what others saw and how he presented himself to others. Scotty was clean and polished outside, like a new garbage can. Inside, stinky garbage. Or like a white-washed tomb—clean and white on the outside with death and decay on the inside. His attitude about everything had become nasty and negative. For Scotty, the glass was always half empty and never half full. There were no grey areas for him; everything was black or white, and if there was a grey area, it was a lie.

Maybe I was drawn to him because we were total opposites, and I could live my dark side through him. For example, I preferred not to say anything if it meant hurting someone's feelings. On the other hand, Scotty felt if it was the truth, he would say it, even if it hurt someone, and he was aggressive and critical. I was assertive and honest, saying something positive before I said anything necessary. He got pleasure from hurting people and used the "I'm telling it how I see it" statement to justify hurting others.

The thing is that it was Scotty's truth, whether it made sense or not. His perspective was always correct, and his truth was the only truth. If he said a situation was a certain way, that's how it was supposed to be, even if one hundred others saw it differently.

Looking back, I believe Scotty was setting me up to believe what he said, that he had changed since becoming a Christian. He was honest and direct and didn't bite his tongue; he said what he meant and meant what he said.

On our first three dates, he vowed to be honest and upfront with me and told me about his relationships with his ex-wives and ex-girl-friends, so if I heard anything differently, I would not believe it because he had already shared with me what *really* happened. You know how it is; we believe the side of the story we hear first. The person who tells the second part of the story or their side has to prove the first person's version is untrue.

It worked for me. When I met and talked to two women who had dated him, my thoughts immediately flashed to what he had told me about them. Neither of the ladies said anything about him after hearing I was engaged.

But, if one had told me not to trust him, I would not have believed them. I had to find out for myself. Scotty had convinced me of what a fantastic catch he was and how good he was to his women. They didn't appreciate him. Common sense should have popped up and reminded me that anyone who brags has dimmed their spiritual light.

Kindness, generosity, respectfulness, and lovingness will be evident. You don't have to brag about it or toot your own horn.

But you cannot see the forest for the trees when caught up in the web of deception and lies. I had been spun into Scotty's lies, believed I loved him, believed he loved me, and wouldn't let anyone say anything negative about my man.

He was an expert in his game, I must say. He had brainwashed me skillfully, planting subtle statements here and there during the first stages of the relationship: "I don't pretend. I'm for real. What you see is what you get. I'm an honest and direct person. I believe in talking about issues. We'll be fine if we don't let a third party nosey around in our business. What goes on in our house stays in our house. I take care of my family. We should always tell each other daily that we love each other because anything can happen when you're apart. I say what I mean. I don't mince my words. We should not go to sleep angry with each other because we might not wake up the next morning. I don't think the wife should have to do all the cooking, cleaning, and housework; we should do it together."

And the biggest one of all, "I know I'm a good man and was a good husband."

Any woman would want to hear her man saying those statements, which sounded pleasing to me.

I guess it's true that you can hear something so many times and so often that you begin to believe it. Scotty's reality became my truth.

Chapter Thirty-Six

IGNORING THE HOLY SPIRIT'S WARNINGS

As Satan's spiritual son, Scotty was slowly stealing my individuality, killing my personality, and destroying my relationship with God, family, and friends.

I stopped socializing with friends as often as I used to because I was always afraid Scotty would do something to embarrass me, or we would fight for the next several months about some male who smiled at me.

Because I didn't consent to all of his whims, Scotty frequently told me I wasn't a Christian. I still attended his church after my Sunday service, but Scotty didn't want me going to my church anymore for some reason.

On Sunday mornings, he'd call and start arguments to upset me, hoping I wouldn't go to my church service. Eventually, I realized this was one of his games and that my week was more hectic when I didn't attend both services. So I didn't let his quarreling keep me from going to church, fellowshipping with other saints, and thanking God for the wisdom to go through what He, Jehovah, was putting me through to strengthen my faith.

As I reflect, I see the Holy Spirit telling me things and showing me issues about Scotty, signals to let me know I shouldn't marry him and that we were unequally yoked, even if he was a churchgoing man professing to be a Christian. But I didn't listen. I didn't heed the warnings and disobeyed the Holy Spirit's guidance. As my mom would say, I was hard-headed. And I suffered the consequences of my actions.

The Holy Spirit almost slapped me in the face with signs that Scotty was not my God-given mate. The Holy Spirit did everything but snatch me away from Scotty and lead me out of the relationship. But I had to do it my way. I guess I hadn't been abused, misused, mistreated, disrespected, and dishonored enough yet.

I was waiting for God to remove Scotty from my life, but God didn't bring him into my life. Through lust and loneliness, I opened the door to Satan and Scotty. It would be more than two years before I realized I was the only one who could remove him from my life.

Here is an excellent example of Satan's manipulation of our minds. Scotty had called me prideful, stubborn, and insecure with low self-esteem. He accused *me* of being a poor listener and arrogant so often that I took on those traits internally and started praying for God to remove them from me and make me more like Scotty wanted me to be.

Instead of stopping the madness in my life, I prayed for God to change me. "Lord, show me how to control my temper and emotions." Scotty was the one with the quick temper and erratic emotions. "Father, help me to control my tongue." Scotty was the one with the sharp tongue. "Jesus, help me to be more humble, meek, teachable, coachable, submissive, and tolerant."

Scotty said I didn't have those traits, and I prayed to have them.

Of course, I didn't realize I was praying against myself then. I knew I wasn't perfect and could improve in many areas, but no one had ever told me I was intolerant, impatient, arrogant, prideful, stubborn, insecure, or had low self-esteem in the forty years I had been on this earth. But when Scotty named it, I claimed it, trying very hard to please him and be the clone he wanted me to be, losing my identity.

I was antsy, fidgety, and frustrated with him, but I couldn't sever the relationship permanently. Sure, I'd break up with him, and after several days of his calls, gifts, and "I love you," we would be back together.

The facts were that he chose not to buy the engagement ring he and I initially decided on, saying he didn't have the money, which I don't believe. His transportation and DME business were raking in cash.

He didn't know I knew of the shady deals he and Moses did to make money. He tricked seniors into giving them their Medicare numbers, billed Medicare for equipment and services never provided, and billed higher rates for their Medicare transportation service.

Chapter Thirty-Seven

FROM THE CROCK-POT TO THE FRYING PAN

I realized something was seriously wrong in our relationship and began acknowledging that I was not hearing and seeing with my spiritual ears and eyes. But I couldn't get off the merry-go-round and was going to the crock-pot from the frying pan.

I sometimes wonder if Scotty had some spell on me. He said he saw a psychic daily for twenty years but stopped seeing her when he joined the church. While looking for towels at his house, I found some curse books with demons, gargoyles, snakes, and upside-down crosses hidden underneath the towels.

The thought crossed that he had put a spell on me with the food he prepared or with the psychic. But I shrugged it off as I did everything else.

I was still hoping for someone else to get me out of the dire situation I had gotten myself into, somehow deceiving myself into thinking that counseling with a preacher would solve our problems. I discovered that discussing issues and not doing anything about them is fruitless.

I thought Scotty would be more honest and receptive if we talked to his pastors. After four weeks of counseling and talking about many issues, you get it: *discussing* problems but never resolving any issues between us.

We agreed that bringing negative baggage from past relationships could affect our relationship. In the same breath, Scotty stated vehemently that neither his past marriages nor his upbringing had anything to do with our relationship and would not affect our marriage. Most would agree that baggage from our past can cause issues with honesty, hurt, anger, resentment, and bitterness if not dealt with properly.

At one of the sessions, Scotty stated that he did not believe the wife should communicate with her ex-husband or his family, not just the ex-husband, mind you, but none of the ex-husband's family. I tried to help him to understand that we divorced our spouses, not their families. He was adamant that I would contact my ex-husband through his family.

Scotty also said I should throw away all pictures and memorabilia attached to old boyfriends, stating, "I don't believe in keeping reminders and memories of old relationships. That's your way of remembering and reminiscing about your old flames."

"That's ridiculous, Scotty. My in-laws are my son's family and part of him."

"See, you just said, "In-laws and not ex-in-laws."

A sad sigh came loud, and I glanced at the pastors, who said nothing.

To me, that was fanatical and bizarre thinking. Am I the person off base here? Should you stop communicating with your child's relatives just because you're marrying someone else? Should you destroy all your memories just because you're marrying someone insecure? Is looking at pictures of old vacations, weddings, and graduations with old boyfriends reminiscing about the old boyfriend?

I kept telling myself Scotty could not be that hateful and insecure, and I could sway him to my thinking. I kept telling myself he would change after we were married and realized that I married him, not the other men. I kept telling myself he would learn nothing was wrong with maintaining pictures of me with old boyfriends.

After all, they were only pictures. I kept pictures to remember the occasion and location I'd visited more than trying to recall the men I'd dated.

I was totally and completely incorrect! Scotty didn't change his opinion one iota after the weeks of counseling, and I kept praying for God to change him instead of fleeing from the relationship and running as fast as I could in the opposite direction.

The stress created by Scotty started physical reactions in my body – headaches daily, elevated blood pressure, shrinking of my urethra, making me unable to urinate, and constipation. I was getting fatter and fatter each day from the pre-cooked dinners he prepared. By our wedding day, I had gained fifty pounds.

One day, I absentmindedly said, "I've got to lose this extra weight."

He responded, "You're never going to lose that weight; you have no discipline."

He loved me being a couch potato and getting fat. It gave him one more thing to use to put me down. He kept my favorite junk foods in his house and told me I should use self-control. He was such a supportive person and gave me such motivation. Ha! Ha!

When the Holy Spirit couldn't grab my attention while I was awake, He tried to warn me in my dreams. I remember this dream like it happened yesterday. Deathly afraid of snakes, even dead ones, I had this realistic dream about a snake with no head or tail.

Around 4:00 a.m., I awoke shaky, perspiring, and fearful from this dream of holding a snake's body in my hands. The reptile didn't have a head or a tail, and I was screaming for someone to bring me a bag to drop the snake in. The louder I called, the larger and more powerful the snake grew in my hands, wrestling hard to free itself.

Withstanding my fear and with all my strength and fortitude, I held onto the wriggling snake until someone brought me a clear plastic bag. I threw the creature into the bag and tied it securely. Once in the bag, the serpent grew two heads on the opposite ends of its body with huge, glaring, demonic eyes staring at me through the bag.

My body shuddered from the hateful, frightening stare, sending pain into my bones.

I believe the dream was a revelation of Scotty. The body of the snake with no head was me holding on to a relationship with no significance, wholeness, or life to it. The more frustrated and fearful I became with Scotty, the more abusive and controlling he became.

The two heads were the two sides of Scotty I saw—the charming, overprotective, caring side and the jealous, vindictive, bitter, spiteful side.

The big, mean, hateful, demonic eyes staring were Scotty's intimidation. He would often stare as the snake did in my dream, with a look of disgust and evil in his eyes.

"For, as he thinks in his heart, so is he" Proverbs 23:7 (Amplified).

That was a good quote for me to remember. "As he thinks in his heart, so is he"—hateful, hostile, bitter, angry, envious, jealous, suspicious, doubtful, fearful, unforgiving, spiteful, resentful, vindictive, and evil thoughts; or loving, kind, forgiving, faithful, trusting, and positive reviews. Scotty had all of the characteristics in the first ca tegory.

Still praying for God's plan for my life, my feelings were edgy and shaky regarding marrying Scotty. I asked God to reveal his divine will, open my spiritual eyes so I could see the direction He desired for me to go, and open my spiritual ears so I could hear distinctly the guidance Yahweh revealed to me through others and his Word. I prayed to Jehovah to open my spiritual mind to comprehend His wisdom's breadth, depth, and width. I wanted a clear spiritual heart to believe and receive all God had promised me.

I prayed to God but didn't listen to the Holy Spirit when he guided me.

Chapter Thirty-Eight

THE WEDDING DAY

Granted, Scotty still had good points, but the verbal assaults, arguments, jealousy, mistrust, vengefulness, judgment, and critical attitude far outweighed his good.

Yet, I still felt compelled to marry Scotty; convincing myself that his mental health issues caused the bizarre behaviors, and he would get better if he took his meds as ordered.

We even had a massive argument on our wedding day regarding my plans to keep my ex-husband's last name. Not thinking it would be an issue hyphenating my last name since Brian would still be my new last name, I didn't know to discuss it with Scotty, naively thinking that becoming his wife was more important than the previous name.

Scotty shouted, "See, there you go, being manipulative in not discussing that you wanted to keep your first husband's name in our pre-marital counseling."

"I didn't think of discussing changes to my last name because I didn't think it would be an issue." I glanced at the pastor and then Scotty. "I didn't think it would be such a big deal. I've still got your last name."

Scotty snarled, "I'll be darned if I have another man's name on my marriage license. I'll call the wedding off before I allow another man's last name to be on my marriage license. I don't care what you say,

Hannah; if Jesus came down himself and told me it's okay for you to keep another man's last name, I wouldn't do it!"

That should have been a flashing warning for me regarding his Christianity. He told me he would not obey Jesus, whom he professed to serve, honor, and obey.

His eyes didn't blink as he stared at me. "I'm not having another man's name on my marriage certificate." He kicked a chair over and stormed out of the room.

My body started trembling uncontrollably, and I tried to maintain composure in front of Scotty's pastor, who gazed at me with kindness before leaving on Scotty's heels. Although I fought hard to keep back the tears, they came anyway. I had had the last name Cotton for fifteen years. I built my career and business using my first husband's last name. Crying tears of sorrow and ruining my make-up, I determined canceling the wedding over the last name would be unreasonable. Adamant that I didn't want Satan to win the victory by causing me not to marry the man I felt destined to unite with because of something as trivial as a name on the marriage license, I swiped the tears and gave in, yet again to Scotty's demand.

Satan manipulated me into marrying Scotty by making me feel guilty if I called off the wedding over the last name.

We had a church full of family and a few close friends. Some relatives had come in from out of the state to surprise us. I didn't know what to do. At any rate, we almost called the wedding off.

I wish I had called Scotty's bluff. He had a pair, and I had a royal flush, mucking when I should have called his bluff or raised my bet. I was so confused, with tears dripping, my head tilted, and my eyebrows furrowed. I blamed Satan for the drama on my wedding day instead of thinking the Holy Spirit may have given me one last warning before jumping into the fiery furnace.

To add to my despair, I overheard Charlessa's mom talking to another guest. "Hannah is quite a lady to marry that fool. I lived with him for three years, knowing he had a demonic spirit. He beat me when I was eight months pregnant, and when I put him out, he called my job and told them I was a drug addict and a drug dealer. Because of his lie, I had to do random drug screens for a year. He is meaner than a junkyard dog and doesn't get along with anyone. He pulled a gun on my brother because he defended me during one of our fights and threatened to kill him if he ever returned to our house. The music is playing; we'd better return to the sanctuary."

I dashed back into the dressing room. *That was before Scotty was a Christian. He has changed a lot since then. I can't call the wedding off because of gossip. Why is she even here?*

With my son escorting me, I strolled down the aisle with a broad grin and stood beside Scotty. When I smiled at Scotty, beady, cold, emotionless eyes stared back, his jaws drooping like a mean bulldog. As I stood there, it dawned that it was the same stare the snake had given me in the dream. I wanted to turn and run, but my feet stuck to the floor like concrete.

Scotty didn't smile once during the ceremony. He had gotten his bride, but his heart wasn't in the nuptials.

I was in the Twilight Zone, going through the motions but feeling like I was in a nightmare I couldn't wake from.

When the minister asked, "If anyone has just cause why this couple should not be married, speak now or forever hold your peace."

We were stunned to hear a male voice reply, "The man is a maniac, and Hannah must be crazy too if she marries him."

All heads turned toward the back of the church, and there stood Lenny, unshaven, wide-eyed, unkempt, and like he hadn't changed clothes in weeks. "That maniac held me hostage in his basement and tried to kill me. Hannah, tell them! What type of spell does he have on you? Tell them, Hannah! You know I'm telling the truth! I'm trying to save your life!"

Still speechless and frozen like an ice carving, I opened my mouth to speak, but no words came out.

The guests gazed from the altar to Lenny, captivated, as though they were watching a video presentation.

Scotty shouted as he walked toward the rear of the church, leaning on his cane, "Get out of here! Did Hannah invite you?"

Lenny pulled a gun from his blazer pocket and shouted, "It's payback time, Mr. Brian. Now, I have the gun, and I'm in control. I don't mind returning to prison either, and I won't miss like you did. Fall on your knees and beg for your life; maybe I'll be merciful."

Two of Scotty's nephews came inside from smoking and saw Lenny with the gun pointed toward their uncle. They sneaked behind Lenny; one put Lenny in a chokehold while the other nephew twisted the gun out of his hand. As they wrestled Lenny to the floor, the guests awoke out of their trance and shouted, "Call the police! Call 911!"

Two police officers took Lenny away, and the ceremony continued with the question from the minister. "If anyone has just cause why this couple should not be married, speak now or forever hold your peace."

Everyone else was quiet as a church mouse. You could have heard a spider weaving a web if you had listened closely enough.

After the ceremony, I was happy as a new bride. I thought the issue of me using my son's last name was done and over with, but Scotty was fuming. His eyes squinted, and his jaws clenched throughout the wedding dinner. I expected his wrath to be about Lenny's appearance at our wedding, not more questions regarding my wanting to keep my first husband's last name.

Scotty feigned pain in his back, hip, and knees and didn't want to go to the lakefront, planetarium, or park to take outside pictures. We didn't go on a honeymoon because he had surgery scheduled the week after the ceremony. He was non-talkative on the ride home. I tried to make conversation, "The ceremony was nice, don't you think so?"

His reply was, "Uh huh."

"We had more people than we invited. I guess family members told others, and they wanted to celebrate with us."

His head nodded, but he said nothing.

A knot tightened in my stomach and in my spirit. I felt something was up, but I had no idea he was still so angry about the last name issue. Before I could unlock the door for us to enter the house, he began quarreling about the last name.

"Stop lying, Hannah, and tell me the real reason you wanted to keep your first husband's last name. It doesn't make sense what you said about your career. You should not have married me if you didn't want my last name. Why did you marry me, anyway? You've been lying during this whole relationship. You can't be trusted. We had all those counseling sessions, and you didn't mention the last name once.

"You were hoping to slip it onto the marriage license. You're one lying woman. I don't know why I married you, either. You make me sick to my stomach." He gagged and turned away from me. "You wanted to keep his last name because you still love him. Well, not with me, baby. I've told you many times that I am nobody's fool!"

We argued for two hours on our wedding night, and I was also angry afterward. He wouldn't listen to logic and kept trying to analyze why I wanted my ex-husband's last name, saying what I said didn't make sense. He kept saying it had to be another reason, and if I didn't want his last name, I should not have married him.

It was absurd because I was taking his last name and keeping the last name I had had for over fifteen years, although the marriage only lasted for five. It was a good time to say I shouldn't have married him; we are married now.

After more hours of trying to explain my rationale for wanting to keep my first husband's last name, I flatly stated, "I don't want to discuss it anymore." The doorbell rang as I headed toward the bedroom.

Scotty answered the door. "Good evening," he said to two police officers. "How can I help you?"

"Is it okay if we come inside, sir?" the older officer asked.

Scotty paused, stared at them for a few beats, stepped aside, and waved them inside.

Once inside the living room, the older officer spoke first. "Are you Scotty Brian, and do you have a daughter named Charlessa Brian?"

Scotty's head tilted, and his arms folded across his chest. "Yes."

I listened from the bedroom doorway.

"Is it okay if we sit?" asked the younger officer.

Scotty pointed to the sofa, and he sat on a tan recliner.

The officers sat on the edge of the sofa and looked at Scotty. The older officer said, "I have bad news to tell you." He paused as Scotty's body stiffened, and he slid to the edge of the recliner. "Charlessa was shot today and is dead."

I rushed into the living room as Scotty's body slumped, and he nearly fell off of the chair. "What happened?" I asked. "I'm Mrs. Brian, Scotty's wife."

Scotty composed himself, sat straight, and looked at the police officers. "What happened?"

Compassion in her voice, the younger female officer answered as she stared at Scotty. "We need you to verify the body, but her driver's license and dental records match Charlessa Brian's."

Scotty's tone hardened, and he glared at the female officer. "How was she killed?"

The young officer remained calm. "She was shot in the head at close range, execution style. I'm sorry for your loss."

The color drained from Scotty's face, and he slumped back into the recliner. He put his head in his hand and sobbed as tears flowed down his face. My arms crossed his shoulders, and I hugged and comforted him while he moaned and wept.

The officers waited while Scotty cried, and after a few minutes, the older officer said, "In a couple of hours, you can go to the coroner's office to view the body and retrieve her belongings. Do you have any questions for us?"

Scotty wiped the tears from his face with his hands. "Yes. Why would anyone want to execute my daughter? She didn't do drugs and wasn't a drug dealer."

The female officer spoke. "We think it was retaliation for a drug deal that went bad with the dealer she was living with. We'll get you more information as we obtain it."

"What? My daughter was living with a drug dealer?" Scotty looked down and thought for a beat. "You are lying, or you have the wrong person. Charlessa wasn't staying with no dealer!"

The officers eyed each other, stood, and headed toward the door. The female placed a card in Scotty's hand. "If you have any questions, don't hesitate to call us. When we find out more information, we'll inform you."

The card dropped to the carpet as Scotty's body went limp. I escorted the law persons to the door, thanked them, and returned to the living room, where Scotty slumped in the recliner, sobbing loudly.

After hours of crying, he wiped away the tears. "I guess we just wait for the coroner to call."

A few hours later, we went to the coroner's building to retrieve her belongings and verify Charlessa's body. After the funeral, Scotty vowed to find and kill the drug dealer boyfriend he felt was responsible for Charlessa's death.

After Charlessa's death, he talked less and less to me, became anti-social, and started talking to himself, walking in his sleep and becoming obsessed with meeting Charlessa's boyfriend.

I was married to a man whose sole purpose was to kill two men—one he thought was sleeping with his wife and the other he believed was responsible for his daughter's death.

After the first month of our marriage, I admitted that I had *not* married the man God had destined for me. I had made the biggest mistake in my life. I had not listened to and obeyed the Holy Spirit.

Now, I had to sleep in the bed I made for myself. I remembered a saying from an auntie, "If you lie down with a dog, you may rise with fleas."

Feeling I couldn't scripturally divorce Scotty simply because the scales had fallen off my eyes, I determined to stay in the marriage, be a holy and virtuous wife, and pray for God to change Scotty and me into the godly husband and wife described in the Bible.

Bedeviled. Bewitched. Voo-dooed. Hexed; damned in the marriage to the man I felt was Satan's son.

Unless God intervened, I was bound in a nefarious marriage for life.

LEAVE A REVIEW

I would love to read what you thought of Bedeviled. You can write a review with your thoughts at:

Amazon

Goodreads

Facebook

Connect with the author:

Website: www.bhcarterauthor.com

Email: barbara@bhcarterauthor.com

Instagram: www.instagram.com/bh_carterauthor

Twitter: www.twitter.com/bh_Carterauthor

FB: www.facebook.com/BHCarterMinistry

SNEAK PEEK

Turn the page for a sneak peek to learn more about Scotty's devilishment in the sequel.

WORMWOOD MARRIAGE

Available summer 2024

WHAT HAPPENED TO THE HONEYMOON

I picked up voices as I stepped into the living room.

Since watching television shows like Jerry Springer or Maury Povich was Scotty's most enjoyable activity, I assumed the voices came from the TV in the back. When I walked into the bedroom, no Scotty was visible or television playing. I must be hearing things. I could have sworn that I heard voices.

My hands went to my hips. "Satan, you're not messing with my mind. I bind you in the name of Jesus!" I mumbled under my breath as I searched for Scotty.

While I strolled back to the living room, Scotty's voice boomed clearly from the deck. I heard my new husband communicating with his dead daughter, "Charlessa, you can come back. You're daddy's girl, and I miss you very much. My psychic says you're resisting."

My hand went over my mouth, and I stepped back, my purse and keys dropping onto the sofa table. A spirit of fear and apprehension temporarily gripped me, and I stood motionless like a chunk of marble. I had been married to the man I now felt was Satan's son for four weeks before observing his bizarre behaviors.

I stated softly but boldly, *"He who is in me is greater than he who is in the world"* John 4:4 (RSV).

I weighed my options. Should I go out to the deck? What if he has conjured up an evil spirit? Do I want to do spiritual warfare?

Still posed like a chiseled statue, glaring toward the deck, trying to spot Scotty, my head spun, and I fell against the wall. We'd only been married for a month, and my new husband sat on our deck talking to a dead person.

I had to think fast before he or his companion spirits sensed my presence. Should I confront or avoid it? Avoidance was painless, so I chose to leave. I picked up my purse and keys, stealthily tiptoed back to the front door, opened it without a screech, and slammed it shut loudly.

Galumph!

I re-entered, strolled into the living room, toward the dining room, and Scotty waved from the deck. I approached him, pecked his lips, and asked what he was doing.

"Nothing." His eyes twitched, and he slid a black book with gargoyles and upside-down crosses on the front cover into his pocket. "It was such a beautiful day that I decided to get some sunshine on the deck."

My arms crossed my chest. "I thought I heard talking coming from the deck," I said in my singsong voice.

A sideways glance from him caused my arms to drop to my sides, and my face tilted toward the wooden floor.

"You must be losing your mind, Hannah. As you can see, no one is out here but me, so you definitely didn't hear talking."

A close-lipped smile froze on my face. I'm not going to start an argument. I know what I heard, and it was not in my mind.

I decided to change the subject. "What do you want for dinner?" My eyes lifted to meet his gaze, wondering if my spirit would spot any evil in his eyes.

"I don't care." His shoulders shrugged. "Whatever you put together will be okay with me."

After preparing a quick meal of broiled T-bone steaks, salads, and baked potatoes, we ate silently. Afterward, I rushed off to my second job at the school.

Unbeknownst to me, until his psychic called to reschedule an appointment, Scotty had resumed seeing her after Charlessa's death. By eavesdropping, I discovered he saw her daily and participated in witchcraft and séances, trying to bring his daughter back.

After discovering that he was seeing a psychic, I read the eleventh chapter of Luke to him many times until he flatly told me he didn't want to hear them. Without causing him to say I thought I was a know-it-all, with humility and a soft voice, after reading the scriptures, I tried to show how he was opening himself up for more wicked imps to enter his spirit.

"When the unclean spirit is gone out of a man, he walketh through dry places, seeking rest; and finding none, he saith, I will return unto my house whence I came out. And when he cometh, he findeth it swept and garnished. Then goeth he, and taketh to him seven other spirits more wicked than himself; and they enter in, and dwell there: and the last state of the man is worse than the first" Luke 11: 24-26 (KJV).

But Scotty wouldn't listen to me because he didn't think I knew anything about the Bible. We studied the Bible together when we dated, and he enjoyed my interpretations. Now, Scotty said I was a hypocritical Christian. So, obviously, he wouldn't receive what I was trying to impart to him.

The last time he listened to me explain the verses, he'd said, "I saw a psychic every day for twenty years when I was younger, and I'm no worse off for it. I stopped seeing her for many years because things were going well, and I didn't need her. I need her guidance now." He rolled his eyes. "My life seems to be turning to soot, and she is the only one who can help me get back on track. So, stop reading me those scriptures. I know the scriptures better than you do, so I don't need you trying to instruct me, okay?"

I thought, Yeah, as Satan's son, you probably know the scriptures better than I do – you just don't live them.

Scriptures from the gospel of Matthew and Luke came to mind. When the Spirit led Jesus into the wilderness to be tempted by the devil, Satan used the scriptures to try to tempt Jesus, so Satan knows the scriptures.

Scotty scarcely communicated with me since his daughter's death, and the only way I could find out what was happening in his life, which also affected my life, was to listen in on his conversations.

Besides enjoying Springer and Povich, programs that appeared to degrade women, parading most as cheaters, adulterers, or gold-diggers, Scotty was also addicted to Crossing Over and Ghost Whisperer. These TV sites were shows that facilitated communications between the living and the dead, presenting the dead as still being among the living.

After the first incident of hearing Scotty talking to Charlessa, multiple times when I came home early, he conversed with her as if she was still alive. He spoke to her in the hallway, on the deck, but mostly in our bedroom. Scotty spent most of his time isolated. He ate, slept, and spent his day locked away in the bedroom, if not at his medical equipment and transportation business. He even gave up all of his board positions but one.

More familiar spirits attached themselves to Scotty after he opened the door through psychic involvement and witchcraft. He was destroying himself and his life by dabbling in the occult, but he wouldn't listen to our pastors or me. As his wife, I felt obligated to remind him what our pastor and many other preachers said happens when we open our spiritual door for demonic spirits to enter. Of course, my words fell on deaf ears.

Still obsessed with killing Lenny, the man Scotty thought was sleeping with me, he was even more fixated on killing the man he thought was responsible for his daughter's death.

Dipping into his retirement funds, he hired a private investigator to discover everything about Charlessa's former boyfriend. He found that his name was Boston Matheson, but his cronies called him BM, for Boss Man and Big Man.

Boston turned out to be more notorious and high-ranking than Scotty expected. Having started as a Chicago gang leader, he had maneuvered his way into a respectable position. According to Scotty, Boston Matheson was a handsome, intelligent, charismatic drug dealer with a Master of Business Administration from Northwestern University. Wealthy adoptive parents had raised him; the Chicago media frequently connected their names to organized crime.

Scotty mumbled as he re-read the report, "This picture don't look like the dude I saw her out with, and he don't look like no dealer." His mouth twisted to the left. "She must have been living with someone else."

My shoulders just shrugged because I had not met her boyfriend.

After studying Boston's picture for several days, Scotty said during dinner, "I may have seen Charlessa with this dude a few times, but she never said he was her boyfriend or that they were living together."

He took his glasses off and studied the photo. "Yeah, I think this *is* the man I saw her shopping with."

His chin dropped to one shoulder; he said, "This dude lives in Chi-town, and Charlessa had an apartment in Madison."

His brows creased as he pinched the bridge of his nose. "I'm gonna get to the bottom of this."

DEDICATION

I devote this book to my creator and maker, God; to my high priest, intercessor, brother, friend, and Lord, Jesus Christ; and to my comforter, teacher, and guide, the Holy Spirit.

I commit this book to my mother and friend, Estella Kincaid Harvey, who has always encouraged me in whatever I attempted to do. If it had not been for my mother occasionally asking me how my book was coming along, I might never have written this book.

I take pride in dedicating this book to my son, Darrin O. Carter, who has always been there for me. He has so much confidence in me and believes what I always taught him: that you can be whatever you desire and do whatever you choose to do if you put God first.

Lastly, I apportion this book to the memory of my sisters, Elnora Harvey Wilson and Susie Harvey Davis, who were champions in promoting and supporting the family.

ACKNOWLEDGMENTS

I want to thank my sister, Joyce Harvey Davis, for being my unofficial editor, reading and rereading each draft, and giving me insightful and beneficial suggestions to help make this novel flow and transition into Bedeviled.

ABOUT THE AUTHOR

Barbara Harvey Carter is a retired registered nurse residing in Texas. She has spent more than two decades as an addictions counselor, group facilitator, trainer, and healthcare professional in the medical and mental health specialties. Having worked with domestic abuse clients in her professional career and experienced the assaults of abuse, Barbara is knowledgeable and empathetic to the needs of abused women. She believes in women's empowerment and supporting females in their endeavors. She also promoted holistic health – mind, body, and soul – as co-owner of SB Fitness Health Club for several years.

Before relocating, she volunteered as an intercessor, encourager, teacher, and planner at religious, community, and professional organizations. Besides being a fiction Christian author who writes about relationships, the supernatural, and the paranormal, Barbara enjoys spending time with her Lord, Jesus Christ, her son, Darrin, daughter-in-love, Melody, grandchildren Tarrin, Kameron, Jaylen, and her extended family.